The
GOAT

ROGER L. SIMON

Green Hills Books – Nashville, TN
© 2019 by Roger L. Simon

This is a work of fiction. Names, characters, places, and incidents are the product of the author's imagination, or are used fictitiously. Any resemblance to actual persons, living or dead, events, or locales, is entirely coincidental.

First American edition published by Green Hills Books.

FIRST AMERICAN EDITON

ISBN: 978-0-578-51397-3

BY ROGER L. SIMON

BOOKS

Heir
The Mama Tass Manifesto
The Big Fix
Wild Turkey
Peking Duck
California Roll
The Straight Man
Raising the Dead
The Lost Coast
Director's Cut
Turning Right at Hollywood & Vine
I Know Best
The Goat

SCREENPLAYS

The Big Fix
Bustin' Loose (story by Richard Pryor)
My Man Adam
Enemies, A Love Story (with Paul Mazursky)
Scenes from a Mall (with Paul Mazursky)
Prague Duet (with Sheryl Longin)
A Better Life (story)

*For all the tennis players and instructors at the Los Angeles
Tennis Club and the Richland Country Club, Nashville*

I

TURMERIC

The nurse stared down at him. "Hold still," she said.

"You think I can move?"

She didn't smile as she thrust the IV into his arm. One, two, three - when would he feel the blessed opioid relief? He knew it was in disrepute these days, but boy did he need it.

All this for a game of tennis?

If only he had taken the turmeric, Dan Gelber thought. It was supposed to have all those anti-inflammatory properties. Not that he knew it would have helped. He would have needed a clone for that, another Dan to observe the twice a day regimen recommended on the bottle, swallowing those horse-sized pills he never bothered to break in half, as he should have. He suspected it was New Age nonsense anyway. Okay ancient New Age nonsense at this point. Still, it might have been something. Something to avoid the ignominy.

An hour or two earlier - who counted in these circumstances - he was standing on court one at the Hancock Tennis Club. He was in the finals in the age seventy and over tournament, his first time in the final round of anything that he could remember. But better late than never, no?

He was only in the third game of the first set. The score was 1-1, his serve, 30-15 in his favor, not bad so far, even though the 15 was an embarrassing tanked overhead anyone should have made, especially in the finals, when he reached for a ball and it happened—instant agony, electro-shock treatment without the plug. He collapsed to the ground, a hard acrylic over concrete, a coursing pain running down his spine, into his left thigh, down the leg all the way to his big toe. There was a burning sensation he had never felt before. Well, not completely. Some of it he had experienced before—in a bout with sciatica a couple of years back. But this was different, 8.9 to 4.5 on the Richter Scale, if that was an apt comparison. And since this was Southern California, no doubt it was.

This time he was virtually immobile. He wondered for a moment if he would ever move again. Could he even have broken his back? But he had fallen directly on the left glute and then to the ground supine. A break wasn't likely but it didn't stop him from worrying. Breathe, breathe, he told himself, but his lungs weren't responding. Would he ever walk again? Or was it really a coronary this time?

The other players had gathered around him. They were all solicitous—some had been through this themselves—although Dan Gelber had no right to ask such gracious behavior of them given his own habits of mind. Like many his age, or so he assumed, he had watched with mixed emotions as his contemporaries had succumbed to various physical maladies, distended knees, elbow issues, shoulder dislocations, persistent nerve pain that overwhelmed their lives. Usually he was sympathetic, or tried to be, but on other occasions he found himself engaging in a disturbing schadenfreude. There but for the grace of God, he would think, as others hobbled off the tennis court, forever beaten, never to return, one less opponent to deal with in the great game of life of which tennis was only one minor component, yet significant as a symbol of survival of the ever-degenerating fittest. He didn't like himself for those thoughts, even, on occasion, was disgusted by them, but there they were. Worse, on other occasions and hating himself for it, he had felt relieved when his contemporaries had actually expired. Somehow his number had not been called. Might his luck continue.

But now, as the event, or insult, as it was called medically, was happening to him, it was difficult to follow what the other players were saying or even to focus on their faces, let alone thinking. One of them was Ben, his partner with whom he had lost in several tournaments before, but this was to be their big chance after they had won the semis with surprising ease. He couldn't for the moment remember the names of the other guys, his opponents. Oh, yes, Herbert and Manfred. Manfred was from Brazil but had a German name. Good forehand but erratic. An over hitter, he and Ben had agreed. They would favor him, not that it mattered now.

Behind Manfred, some people, club members watching the final, had stood up from the viewing stand and were approaching, a couple talking animatedly into cellphones. Someone reached over to take his pulse.

And then he passed out.

The next thing he knew he was in one of those fire department ambulances, the shiny red ones in that deliberately retro boxy style that seemed designed to carry you over to the other side—the River Styx Special. He had been in one before when he thought he had a heart attack, but it turned out to have been indigestion. He realized the mistake that time halfway to the hospital and tried to get them to turn back, but the medics wouldn't allow it. Against regulations. They made sure he took his aspirin and continued on. So he spent the night in a now defunct hospital in Century City, receiving a bill on checkout that would have paid for a week at the Georges V with a first class flight to Paris, maybe even a private jet, thrown in. His insurance paid a tenth of it and the rest got mysteriously erased.

On this occasion indeed it was different. When he woke up several hours later, it was dark out. Another nurse was staring at him.

"The orthopedist will see you soon."

Soon evidently meant fifteen hours. The orthopedist arrived just before lunch the next day. His name was Dr. Chung and he seemed to be Korean, but did not speak with an accent. Behind him, an elderly cleaning lady who looked Indian or Pakistani was swabbing the floor with a mop.

Amanda was already there. She had come in around ten a.m. with a croissant and a grande-sized almond latte. She knew Dan liked almond milk because they had spent one night together at a hotel in Newport Beach and ordered room service breakfast. But that was a couple of months ago and the relationship had gone nowhere. Dan didn't like admitting it to himself, but when she had taken her clothes off for the first time that weekend, revealing her sixty something skin, well-tended as it was, all Dan could think of was how old he must have looked. Still, it was nice of her to come to the hospital, if a tad embarrassing. His actual family was not in evidence, not that there were many of them. He had been divorced for twenty-three years and his only son lived across the country with his wife and two children. It had seemed pointless to call him and it had never been Dan Gelber's natural way to reach out. He wasn't passive-aggressive exactly so much as self-involved. Amanda's manner appeared to be the opposite. She was the kind of woman who was born bearing responsibility for anyone with the slightest discomfort—and Gelber's was, at this particular moment, more extreme than he could remember it ever having been.

She spread some preserve on the croissant and handed it to him.

"It's blueberry. They were out of the blackberry," she said, again knowing his favorite.

"Are you the spouse?" the doctor asked her.

"Just a friend."

The doctor nodded and bent over to examine Dan, palpating his gluteus and lower back. There was a sharp pain and Dan winced. "How'd this happen?"

"Tennis. Stooping for a ball. Didn't bend at the knees, I guess."

"Not sure that would've helped. Your MRI shows a severely herniated disc between the fourth and fifth."

"It's been that way for a while. I had a year of PT because of it."

"I've already seen your history. Sorry to say but you'll probably need an operation at this point. You look like a candidate for a laminectomy. No one wants one, but sometimes we have to face reality. That will give you a chance for an active life. You're lucky to have been walking around, let alone playing tennis."

"So I guess I should have taken the turmeric."

"Turmeric?" The young doctor chuckled. "You like Indian food?"

The cleaning lady stopped and looked up.

"Not my favorite. But it's supposed to be a good anti-inflammatory, isn't it?"

"It's the curcumin," Amanda chimed in. "You're supposed to take it with a bit of pepper." One of those women who did yoga three times a week and a liquid cleanse every month, she kept up on those things.

The doctor smiled politely. "It won't hurt you but there's absolutely no evidence turmeric… or the curcumin contained in it… does any of the things they claim it does." He started to input some information in an iPad. "Anyway, buck up. A condition like yours responds well to surgery. Sometimes even an incision of less than an inch or two will do it and you're up again in no time. Though I'm not sure tennis will be on the calendar, at least for the time being. Hard courts are murder on the spine. You'll find other ways to exercise. Do you swim?"

"I'm not even sure I can walk."

"You'll walk just fine. You already can. I see you've been to the bathroom twice. Sorry we can't let you stay another night. The nurse will give you some Vicodin." He put his card on the end table. "Call my office tomorrow and we'll schedule an appointment for the operation."

"It'll be something to write about," Amanda added helpfully.

"You're a writer?" the doctor asked. "Anything I should know about?"

"A few books. Some movies. Too long ago for you to have seen them."

"Maybe I watched them on Netflix. My wife loves eighties flicks. 'The Breakfast Club' … 'Sixteen Candles.' You didn't write those, did you?"

Dan shook his head.

"Well, you can tell me when you come in. See you soon I hope. We'll get you fixed up."

The doctor smiled again and headed for the door.

The old Indian woman started to hiss as it closed behind him, as if sending out a curse.

"Don't do operation," she said, turning toward Dan. "Operation terrible. Only get worse. Man here came in with broken toe, had operation, never walked again. Later he die of gangrene. In hospital. Age fifty-two. Left two daughters twelve and fourteen." She resumed mopping, then stopped again, staring back at Dan once more. She seemed to be evaluating him as if to see if he were fit for saving. "Go see Uncle Nawang," she said.

"Who?"

"Nawang Gombo. My cousin. In Reseda. He fix everything - knee, shoulder, hair loss, bad skin, prostate problem, even back. Very good with back. You start dancing soon." She did a little jig by way of illustration.

"Maybe you should," said Amanda. "Operations should always be a last resort." She turned toward the old woman. "Where in Reseda?"

"23393 Erwin Street. In mini mall, next to nail salon."

"Uncle Nawang in a mini mall?" Dan said. "Why not?" He figured he would die first.

II

WESTERN MEDICINE

The operation was a failure. The doctors - there were two beside Dr. Chung - told him not to panic, to give it a few months, but Dan Gelber knew before three weeks had gone by, or thought he did. In fact, he sensed it on his way into the recovery room, not that he could really remember coming out of anesthesia. It was all a blur to him. Yet he could see it in the expressions of the nurses and orderlies - failure, failure, failure. They were trying to be compassionate, but it was compassion that seemed laid on with a putty knife, the kind brought out immediately for emergency use when the procedure had gone disastrously. There was no question that it had this time. He could overhear them muttering about a second operation while he was still half asleep. It had been that way from the start—from the moment the anesthesiologist told him to count back from ten. The guy sounded bizarrely anxious, as if he knew something would go wrong in advance. "Should we be doing this now?" Dan heard him say, gesturing to a television where a news announcer was droning on about the tragedy of the day. Someone was shouting "Get out! Get out!" Before Dan knew what it was or even if it was—maybe the anesthesia, he was assured it was the latest kind, a veritable medical marvel, was already taking effect and he was hallucinating—he was down and out.

Whatever indeed had or did happen, the pain was back the moment he awoke - full force. It only got more severe as the days went on. Normal life turned out to be insufferable. Getting up in the morning was an ordeal taking him what felt like the better part of an hour just to position his feet at the side of the bed so he wouldn't send shock waves up his spine from standing. Brushing his teeth was done slowly, slowly, with a strained meticulousness that might have pleased his dentist at age ten, but now made it feel like half the morning was gone before he even got his coffee. Even pressing the tiny button on the Nespresso machine sent an instant reverberation up his now fused discs.

And then driving - the lifeline of the Angeleno. The first time he sat down at the wheel of his car he did it gingerly, as if he were sliding carefully between the sharp points of some medieval torture device, but the pulsations were excruciating nevertheless - this despite the fancy super-adjustable seats with the extra lumbar support for which he had paid extra, just in case. Well, the case had come and it had failed. The lumbar support felt like an ice pick running up his spine, the deluxe leather seat like a stone stool in a graveyard. Turning the steering wheel was a disaster. His arm strength was gone. Forget about tennis, he could barely open a peanut butter jar. Pulling out of his garage was an ordeal. He had to steer with his left hand because his right had ceased to function altogether. If thy right hand lose its cunning, came the Biblical imprecation. His had. And cunning was the least of it. He had trouble turning on the lights. Walking around, on those rare occasions he could muster up the energy, he looked like a human pretzel, or perhaps the Hunchback of Notre Dame as portrayed by Lon Chaney in the original silent version - a veritable homunculus from the previous century. Who could live a life like that?

Who could indeed because the impetus for that first excruciating drive was the mandatory quarterly visit to his urologist to check his prostate. Dan was on a protocol because three years before he had been diagnosed with prostate cancer, Gleason stage 6. It sounded ominous but he convinced himself it wasn't. The Gleason scale – where did they come up with that name? It reminded him of an episode of The Honeymooners when he was a kid, Jackie Gleason and Art Carney. Away we go, Jackie would say. But this was cancer, not a sitcom. And didn't everyone have it? Didn't all men, well most anyway, show evidence of prostate cancer cells after they were autopsied, almost always having died of something else? Besides he never felt anything. Thus far it didn't affect his life at all. After the first few weeks, he mostly forgot he had it. More importantly, Gleason six wasn't Gleason nine. Nine was trouble. He had been six again the second time they did a biopsy, a process he likened to having a staple gun shot up your ass.

And this time - he found out two days later- he didn't get a nine either. He got a ten. Ten!

Ten only two and a half weeks after an absolutely botched back operation turned him into The Hunchback. The gods were using him as a plaything, tossing him around like a rag doll.

So what, he naturally had to wonder at this point, would happen if actually he did die? Dan Gelber had been one of those people who deliberately avoided thinking about his own death. He would pretend issues of mortality were "above his job description" and lived in a kind of self-imposed oblivion, better to repress thoughts of what everyone knew was inevitable. What could he do about it anyway? But now it was different. Now things didn't quite work. Rigor mortis had reared its ugly head. What if it really was near, not somewhere off at the far end of an actuarial table or something to consider only when reading a tragedy by Shakespeare or Sophocles, something he hadn't done in years anyway? For the first time in his life, Dan Gelber was having trouble suppressing morbid thoughts. What if he did expire, by nature or even by his own hand? Who would arrange for the funeral, make the speeches, call the caterer, try to get at least some kind of obit in the LATimes, some recognition that he had actually *been here*? Amanda? He scarcely deserved her attention, but she would undoubtedly do something. She had brought him sushi twice in the last week, plus – she said he was excused under the circumstances - a cholesterol-laden sandwich from Langer's Deli. They had never been there together but he recalled having mentioned how much he liked their pastrami, a guilty pleasure. Should he put her in his will? That might be excessive, deliver the wrong message. They weren't even really a couple. But come to think of it, where *was* that will? He didn't even remember what it said, hadn't looked at it in decades, since it was changed after the divorce. And even though he had a son with two young grandchildren, one of them with a medical issue of his own, Dan had never bothered to get life insurance. Now he wouldn't qualify. The truth was, although Dan Gelber barely realized it himself, he rarely thought about any of those things until it was too late to do anything about them.

"So, doctor, you taking my prostate out or you going to irradiate it until it shrivels into a raisin? Will my pecker ever get hard again? Will I ever stop peeing? Am I going to have to wear rubber pants, a colostomy bag? What's the story? Give it to me straight. I'm going to kill myself in the next hour, so it doesn't matter."

"I hope you're kidding, Mr. Gelber."

"I hope I am too."

"I have to be honest with you. Considering your condition, some version of those side effects are… more or less likely but…"

"But what?"

"We will do our best to avoid them. And, after a while, you get used to them. You learn to love other things in life."

This time out on the open road, doubled over, barely able to peer over the steering wheel, he was thinking of driving the fucking Beemer off a cliff, right over the edge of Mulholland Drive as many had done before him, drag racing on coke or whatever. A Hollywood death it would be. Maybe it would even get a mention in the trades - retired screenwriter hurtles cliff. No more deals.

He stopped and examined himself in the rear-view mirror. He had never looked older, his complexion ashen, his eyes dull. So this was it? Even after all the deadlifts and squats, the years of hiking Runyon Canyon while swallowing inedible gorp for the promise of eternal life, doing his best to keep booze at a minimum and laying off all drugs but baby aspirin and Lipitor? Well, with a few exceptions, but not many. And he hadn't smoked since high school, except for an occasional cigar to see what all the trendy noise was about, why entertainment lawyers endlessly boasted of their contraband humidors from Havana. And yet he was at the end of his road. Well, he made it to seventy-two, better than some but not most. A white American male was supposed to live to 81.6, according to the actuaries. He could try to go on, but what was the point? To look like this, to be like this? Career finished, no energy, no nothing. Libido at minus 75. No women he cared about anymore, as if he would be the slightest bit attractive to them at this point. Mostly, if not totally, estranged from his family. And tennis - forget that, as if it meant anything in the first place, a mere sport, a game. In other words, life as a hunchback was all that was left. At least he didn't get hit by a bus at age nine like his Aunt Thelma who spent the rest of her lonely spinster days with one arm. A school teacher, she had taught him to parse sentences at the age of seven. She died too young to see the fruits of her labor, that he had become a writer. For a while.

One thing he did tell Thelma about. At the uncommonly young age of fourteen, and with only superficial understanding, he had read

Andre Schwarz-Bart's The Last of the Just, wondering if he were one of the described *lamed vov*, the thirty-six just men, or women, the Biblical Esther said to be one of them, in every generation on whom the survival of humanity depended. These people were so righteous they often didn't even know that they were one of the thirty-six—such things having been debated in endless Talmudic fashion. But they still held the world together, in that novel anyway, from the Twelfth Century English pogroms through the Holocaust. Dan Gelber wanted to be one, or thought he did, when he was young. It made him feel important, superior in some way, even when he discovered there were students in his classes who were just as smart he was, or possibly—gasp—- smarter. Maybe he was a *lamed vovnik*, for all he knew, he told Thelma. Such fantasies were outrageous self-aggrandizement from a fourteen-year old, he now knew, or from anyone, but Thelma just patted his hand and smiled. She understood what life really was about - and that he would see soon enough. The young Dan Gelber didn't realize at the time that he was expressing a need to be unique, to be special, that would plague him all his life.

But why think of that now? The past was a litany of failure punctuated by an occasional success, a torture device designed to make you come back for yet one more spin of the roulette wheel. He did his best to stay away from it, all the excuses and procrastinations. If there was a thing he had come to despise, it was nostalgia and its close cousin self-pity, yet he too often indulged in it. At least he was self-aware enough to know that it was that last chance at the wheel that propelled him on. That and the fact he had always thought suicide a monumentally selfish act, not that he hadn't considered it, as, he assumed, had a solid majority of human beings.

Indeed, he had stood on some rocks above the Hollywood Bowl only a few days before, contemplating a plunge of several hundred feet straight down as he edged ever forward. It would be the most effective way. Pills were useless. People were brought back all the time from an amazing quantity of the seductive little devils to spend months in some dreadful rehab center. And he didn't own a gun. Gas was out of the question, as it was slow and painful. So the swan dive would be the best method, short and sweet. But as he crept forward he knew he couldn't do it. Knew he wouldn't do it. Didn't have the courage. Besides, since suicide had always seemed the most selfish of acts, suicide over a bad, even a miserable, hideously twisted, back seemed almost comically selfish. Even the malignant prostate didn't seem enough.

So, after only a few short weeks, Dan Gelber found himself on a mission - to take what he felt to be the most irrational and desperate of flyers, one he knew was truly absurd. But did he have a choice, any other place to go? Did he want yet another operation to fuse yet more vertebrae that would morph him from a hunchback into a mummy, a rigid barely living corpse to rot away on the couch of his home office, his remains preserved by a dehumidifier turned to high until the stench became so strong it attracted the attention of an overly-persistent FedEx man?

He was already in the Valley, speeding North on Reseda, past half empty strip malls, smog check garages, convenience stores and Armenian bakeries, cities of homeless growing beneath the freeway underpasses, their tents sprouting like toad stools between the weeds, taco stands and falafel joints, Argentinean butchers and halal butchers, tire shops and pawn shops. It was the heart of multicultural Los Angeles, the city most of its inhabitants loved and hated or, more accurately, loved to hate, everywhere and nowhere at once, the melting pot that kept on melting until its contents spilled over into the Pacific on one side and sank into the Mojave on the other, only to discover none of it had ever really come together as one, never fused or united, only existed as isolated dots, one after the other after the other after the other.

He was going to pay a visit to Uncle Nawang.

"In three hundred feet, turn right on Erwin Street," Waze reminded him. The GPS had a slightly twanged accent it called Lightening McQueen, perhaps to conjure Steve, although the actual voice was Owen Wilson's out of Cars 3. "In two hundred feet, your destination will be on your left."

Sure enough, yet another mini mall was before him, most of it shuttered but with the promised nail shop the second window from the right. Something called the International Institute of Hypnotherapy, currently padlocked with the blinds drawn, stood next to a bright red door with words "Ayurvedic Cures - Open 7 Days" printed on it in bright yellow in a handwritten script that looked Hindi or Sanskrit. Dan couldn't tell the difference or, if indeed, it was even one of those two. It was Thai for all he knew.

He pulled into a parking space and gazed straight at the red door for a minute. A broken work light dangled above the jam that looked as if it had been that way for years. What could possibly be inside? This would undoubtedly be the stupidest thing he had done in his life - or at least high among them. But he got out of the car and took a step forward. Man am I ever desperate or out of my mind, Dan Gelber thought. He was from a medical family and could see his father staring up at him in astonishment from the grave. For this I taught you Mendeleev's Table of Elements when you were nine? For this I sat with you at the dining room table when you were in the tenth grade going over proofs in Euclidean geometry? To put yourself in the hands of a South Asian quack in a San Fernando Valley mini mall more than half of whose shops have gone out of business - and for good reason? Sometimes operations don't work out. It's the way of the world. Western medicine, as you know yourself, isn't perfect. But then you try again. You don't give up. You hang in there. All these fruits and berries from the subcontinent may have been of use to the peasantry three thousand years ago, but we live in the modern era. There's a germ theory of disease, antibiotics that work at least some of the time. If you insist on being a California health nut at least go see a licensed chiropractor. I didn't raise you to go to someone who believes in chakras and gives you herbal teas that make you want to vomit from the smell before you even drink - unless of course that's what you want to pretend to be doing to get some ditzy aging flower child in bed. You already had mixed feelings about that. And this is about your life. You only get one of them, I'm sorry to tell you. I know. I'm still dead and I haven't gone anywhere. Not up and not down. Just moldering.

Dan couldn't remember his father ever talking to him that way, but he didn't have to. This was his own version of his father, his own unconscious channeling melded with some distant Mel Brooks routine. The two-thousand-year-old man. Never run for a bus - there'll always be another. But whatever it was, his current undertaking was unqualifiedly nuts. What could he have been thinking?

He turned around and headed back to his car

"Where are you going? You should not be in such hurry."

Dan looked over his shoulder. A man was standing there who at first glance appeared to be in his thirties, but seemed somehow much older. Maybe it was something in the eyes, which were pale blue and almost disappeared in their sockets. He only was about five-four but compact and well-muscled, as if he worked out constantly. He also had light skin for an Indian. Gelber assumed him to be Indian, he certainly had the accent. Indeed, what the man - whom he also assumed to be Gombo - resembled more than anything was older fitness trainers Gelber had seen, men who looked preternaturally young from years of assiduous exercise and careful diet, eighty-year-old faces on twenty-year-old bodies like Jack LaLanne before he died. But he couldn't have been that old. Fifty at the most, possibly fifty-five. Nevertheless, the man made Gelber feel weak and lazy.

"You are Nawang Gombo…"

"Indeed, sir. And you are Dan Gelber. My cousin told me you would be coming."

"She did?"

"She said you have surgery and come after operation fail completely and make you worse."

"Very prescient of her."

"She is that way - my best - how you say - public relations woman … I must inform you do not look good, if you do not mind my saying so."

"Like the Hunchback of Notre Dame."

"Yes, yes, quite so," the man said. There was a twinkle in his pale eyes, but also an odd darkness in the pupils that were jet black. "Bad operations happen so often, particularly for back… Please come in. We will fix you up in no time. Good as new, as they say." The man held open the red door, gesturing Dan through.

"I've got a bum prostate too. I hope you can fix that."

"No problem. No problem."

"Stage ten cancer."

"Ah, not so good. Doctor want to rip it out so you live. Make dick limp like wet lollipop with you peeing all night and day. Never leave toilet." He started laughing but it didn't strike Gelber as funny. "Don't worry. I fix right up."

"How? With some tea or other?"

"Of course. What else? Soon you will be stallion again. Like eighteen but not making stupid mistake."

Dan stared at him. Was he joking? No, of course not. It's what he did. Or thought he did.

The man led Dan down a hall. In a few seconds, they emerged in a surprisingly bright and clean small clinic with a desk, illuminated x-ray panel and several shelves lined with herbs in glass containers. The walls were decorated with illustrations from Ayurvedic medicine and a giant blow-up of a mountain that was so big Gelber immediately assumed it to be Everest. In fact. he was relatively sure since he had seen a sufficient number of images of the world's highest peak as well as the movie of the Edmund Hillary-Tensing Norgay expedition when he was a boy. This was a photograph of a more recent expedition with several Western mountaineers in Winter climbing gear accompanied by Sherpas, some of whom were in similar attire while others were dressed more scantily in traditional costumes One of the latter was Gombo.

"You are Nepali."

"Yes, very much so. On my mother and my father's sides. Though some of my cousins are from Bhutan."

"You're a long way from home."

"Yes, yes. Very much so," he repeated like somebody's gossipy uncle in a Bollywood wedding movie. "Nineteen hours on plane, change in Bangkok for Kathmandu. You will see." He gestured for Gelber to sit down, then walked behind him and began to palpate his shoulders, almost immediately shaking his head. "Very stiff, like solid rock formation in back. North face of Annapurna. My finger ache when I touch. Maybe get calluses. Never do stretches for twenty-five years. I can tell. No doubt you take prednisone... other steroid.... Diclofenac, flexural.... so-called great miracle Western medicine...." He began running his index finger down Gelber's spine now, slowly and carefully as if each vertebra contained Braille messages. "... relieve pain for minute or hour but turn bone into dust in long run. Body collapses like wicked witch on floor." He stopped and looked straight at Dan, frowned. "You spend too much time at desk, hunched over computer. Watching porn on Internet or working long into night on project. You are lawyer?"

"Writer. Sort of retired now."

"Senile?"

"Hope not."

"Then why retire? I am ninety-seven."

"Ninety-seven?!"

Dan took a second - or was it a third - look. They said these days sixty was the new fifty and so forth, but this was beyond belief. Was it some kind of sales scam? Did he purposefully exaggerate his age to entice the customer? Ninety-seven was incredible, impossible, beyond the beyond for someone in his kind of shape, unless he was a living mummy.

"You would like see birth certificate?" said Gombo, staring in amusement at Gelber's nonplussed expression. "Is in Nepalese language, but I can translate."

"No, no, not necessary."

"Good. Wastes time when we must get you better." He took some small canisters off the shelf and started to spoon out some herbs into an envelope. "You make tea three times day, no more than one cup, otherwise acid reflux."

"What is it?"

"Turmeric, resveratrol, vitamin B-12, fish oil."

"I get that on Amazon."

"Ha-ha. Just joking. Are secret ingredients from shaman high in Himalaya. Rhodiola only part, cannot tell you more."

"A real shaman, eh?"

"Yes, most famous healer. From village near Shivapuri. Very big mountain. 3452 meters." He handed Gelber the envelope. "Charge for visit and herb sixty dollar... I am sorry but services not covered by Medicare, although two client get part reimbursement from private secondary insurance. I can give you form."

"Don't bother. Sixty bucks to cure both my frozen back and cancer at the same time seems more than fair - assuming it works. A bargain of bargains, in fact."

"May take several visits.... You can pay cash or credit card. Visa or Master only."

Gelber sniffed the envelope. It smelled worse than a dead skunk he had found in his back yard one summer night during a heat wave and made him throw up before he even reached the garbage cans. Yes, I have gone certifiably mad, he thought as he handed Gombo his credit card.

III

TENNIS, ANYONE?

"**D**an, I can't believe your surgery was only four weeks ago and you're already out on the court," said Jill Raleigh, a well-heeled woman in her early sixties. They were having breakfast on the club's lanai with Amanda. "My ex wouldn't show his face for six months after he had arthroscopic and then he would only appear for the Sunday barbecue after almost everyone had gone home. And then he wanted to come in a trench coat. I wouldn't let him. It was too silly."

"I lost."

"That's because your partner double faulted seven times in three games." That last was whispered in order not to offend Edith Winkler, Dan's mixed doubles partner of the morning, who was seated three tables away. But given the way Jill projected her voice ever so slightly in the end, Dan wasn't sure if the whisper was intended to attract attention in the first place. Women had such complex rivalries they were difficult to follow for a mere male.

"She's right, Dan," Amanda chimed in. "The day before yesterday you were a basket case. You wouldn't even answer the phone."

That was because he was brewing a cup of Gombo's tea when she called. He was on his third day over all, morning and night. But how would she know that?

"And your complexion is so good. You look…" Jill gestured

"Sixty-five," said Dan, tongue half in cheek.

"I was going to say sixty."

"Why not thirty?"

"Okay, thirty."

"Stop it," said Amanda. "You're going to give him the fattest head in the club. And I'm going to have to deal with it. He doesn't look a day over... sixty-two... a young sixty-two."

"I just want to know what he's been using. I've tried every anti-aging cream at Neiman's but not a single one has—"

"Rhodiola."

"What's rhodiola?"

"An adaptogen. At least that's what it says on Google.... An herb that helps the body adapt to stress... normalize bodily processes. Something like that."

The two women looked at each other. "Well, we better get some, whatever it is," said Jill. They both nodded emphatically. For a moment Dan had the unpleasant thought that he was at an assisted living facility, not a tennis club.

"But you can't use it by itself. You need the secret ingredient from a Himalayan shaman. Otherwise it doesn't work at all."

The women started laughing.

"I'm not kidding," he said flatly.

"Sure, sure," said Ben, Dan's regular doubles partner who had just walked up. "Secret ingredient from the Himalayas. Works every time. But is it good for your backhand?" Amanda was suddenly frowning, staring quizzically at Dan, as if recalling something. "It better be," Ben continued, "because I guilted Herbert and Manfred into a makeup match. They get to keep the trophy anyway, but we could win a Pyrrhic victory.... Of course, if you're not up to it...."

Dan hesitated, wondering if this would be too much. This was his first day out and he didn't want to ruin things when they just seemed to be getting better. Meanwhile Amanda was still staring at him, now with a half-smile as if she had a notion of what was the cause of this. She was in the hospital room where it all began, after all. But then who could believe it?

Dan took a moment, gathered himself and stood. Why not? The rematch — or rather the match - would be a test.

If it was, it wasn't much of one. Dan hadn't played better in several years. In fact, he surprised himself, how well he was hitting. He didn't even feel a twinge in the elbow that had nagged him for what seemed like a decade. He and Ben beat their opponents 6-2, 6-2, largely on some excellent serving by Dan who - despite his back surgery - was able to lean way back like a seventeen-year old and, resurrecting his high school American Twist, pinpoint it into Manfred's body. This forced his overeager opponent to over hit again and again and eventually to slam his racquet into the court bench, splitting the frame. He wasn't much more successful with his replacement racquet.

"You played amazingly well, I must say," said Ben as they were heading for the locker room for their shower. "Considering the way I last saw you, 'Like a patient etherized upon a table.'" Ben was a literary type for a lawyer. "I wondered whether you'd ever walk again, let alone wipe out your adversaries. I'm afraid of you in singles now. Maybe you should go on the senior circuit. I better get the name of the surgeon, just in case I need him some day - assuming he's not a Himalayan witch doctor..." he added.

"Oh, but he is. From a village near Shivapuri. That's a very big mountain. 3452 meters."

"Good to know," Ben laughed, hiding what Dan detected to be some impatience with his overextending a seemingly juvenile joke. "Even if my back holds out, I'm going to go see him for my serve and everything else... Will I need oxygen?"

"Altitude pills."

For the first time in what felt like years, Dan was feeling relaxed and at ease with himself as he drove home after the tennis. Did the tea also do that, he wondered with a laugh? Maybe he would lose his edge. He had often thought his abilities as a writer, waning as they might have been, always depended on a certain tension, a need to communicate to the world to prove his life was of some consequence, had some meaning. Otherwise, what was he? That seemed almost silly or at least superfluous for the moment. Life was with people, wasn't it? Speaking of which, he realized then that he hadn't spoken with his son Zack in over a month—or was it two? Probably closer to two. This lack of contact wasn't abnormal. It could have been ascribed to the cliché about being out of sight and therefore out of mind, but it was actually more. His son, who lived in Teaneck, New Jersey, was, though Dan Gelber was loath to admit it, indeed sometimes seriously disliked himself for feeling that way, something of a disappointment to him. Zack was a marketing executive—an occupation Gelber considered lesser in a family of doctors, lawyers and writers—and a junior one at that, although already well up in his thirties. Dan had various explanations—or were they excuses—for what he regarded as this failure on his son's part. Was it the divorce? Was it his mother's occupation? For much of their marriage she had been a "life coach," a metier, Gelber thought, invented for those too lazy to get a real degree in psychology. This disdain—though he endeavored to hide it—had affected the marriage as well. But the more important problem, the one that lingered and still plagued him in his later years, was that Dan Gelber had difficulty letting Zack be Zack, a truly separate person and not an extension of his father. And Zack, on his part, had his own recognition of what his father thought of him, painful though that might be. Nevertheless, both men had for some time made their peace with their relatively alienated relationship. They kept in touch by text and rarely spoke, but on the rare occasions they did, both did their best to keep up a jovial façade.

"Call Zack," Gelber said into his cellphone. His son picked up on the third ring.

"Hey, pop, I'm in a hurry here. Meetings up the yin-yang. But I got your text. It's great the back is feeling better. Linda and I were worried. But what was that about Shivapuri? You're not going all multi-culti, are you? You of all people."

"Don't worry about it. I've been vaccinated against gurus."

"Well, just as long as it hasn't expired." There was a bit of a pause. "Aren't you going to ask about the kids?"

"I thought you were in a hurry." Actually it had slipped his mind. "How're they doing?"

"Samantha wants to quit her cello lessons. I told her she was going to have no chance at an Ivy League college if she does that."

"Good."

"Are you serious? You went to one." There was another silence. "Aren't you going to ask about Peter too?"

"Yes, of course…How's he doing? Better, I hope." Peter was Zack's younger son. He was having attention problems in kindergarten. Or was it nursery school, Dan Gelber wondered? Maybe he was in second grade, for all he knew.

"I think we found the right doctor."

"Well, that's good."

"With the autism center at Beth Israel."

"He's—?"

"Minor. It's minor. They think they can handle it."

"That's great."

"Yes, it's a relief. Look, I gotta run. Glad you're feeling better. Talk over the weekend."

Autism? Dan Gelber hadn't realized it had reached that level. But why would he have, his communication was so intermittent? Well, it was good the boy was getting medical attention. Life was hard for everyone, he consoled himself. It would work out. Who knew—maybe the child would turn out to be exceptional? These things had their way of working out in surprising ways, Dan told himself.

That night Dan had trouble sleeping, though he had taken another cup of the tea that evening, which made seven over all. The back was fine, but his good mood had been destroyed on his ride home. He kept thinking of his grandson Peter, then tried to put him out of his mind. What could Gelber do anyway? He didn't even have a good fix on what the child looked like at this point. Baby pictures, with rare exceptions, all looked the same to him. Besides, now the boy was four and he couldn't remember seeing any recent photos, just some curly brown hair—or was it really dirty blond? He sat up and tried to locate a photo on his iPhone, but it wasn't there. As the night wore on, he couldn't sleep at all, trying to picture Peter in his mind's eye. Evidently, Gombo's potion didn't guarantee equanimity or equalize the emotions after all in any way he could discern. You are on your own in that department. Wasn't that always the case?

He lay in bed for several hours, staring at the ceiling with the distinct sensation that - despite his improved physical condition - something was going astray. Things were changing or slipping away in a manner he couldn't quite define. He was floating in space somewhere yet still supine in bed, a feeling of being out of control like drug experiences he had had years before. He hadn't liked that much then and he liked it even less now. Somewhere around three a.m. he gave up on sleep and got up to go to the bathroom. He stopped short when he noticed himself in the mirror. God, he looked young! Easily the fifty-five Jill had decreed. That number wasn't even flattering. He seemed more like fifty or forty-five. Or even younger, especially around the eyes. The sag was gone and the little droop above his left lid. His complexion seemed less sallow, like the better part of the before and after pictures in those magazine advertisements for the latest skin cleanser - the ones he always wondered why anybody trusted. They seemed such obvious fakes. No skin cream was that good or ultimately had a chance of defying father time. And even if it did, he hadn't used one in the first place.

To check himself he walked into his office for a copy of his most recent book, published, it pained him to recall, almost ten years ago already, when he was in his early sixties. He walked back into the bathroom and held the author photo up next to his own face in the mirror. The discrepancy was remarkable. The living - if that was the word - person looked so much more youthful. How could this be possible? Had Gombo turned him into Dorian Gray? Why wasn't he marketing that tea all over the place? Dan Gelber couldn't decide whether he was dreaming it all or this was real. And since it was three-twenty in the morning, maybe this wasn't the time to make a determination. Finally, he drifted off to sleep.

He woke up late the next morning to text messages from both Jill - who wanted to play tennis (test him in singles, she said) - and Amanda - who wanted to meet for lunch downtown. There was a new sushi bar she wanted to try. He was suddenly quite popular. He couldn't remember the first time two women had texted him at once. If it had ever occurred, such an event would have pre-dated texting by one or two decades. Rousting himself to take a shower he caught another glimpse in the mirror. It wasn't a dream, unless he was still dreaming. He actually pinched himself to make sure. No, he looked like a vigorous man in perhaps young middle age. He indeed would have been quite a catch for Jill or Amanda. Objectively, he looked too young for either of them. In fact, he wondered how he would go back to the club. People would think he had some kind of extreme face lift, not exactly his style. Or gone Botox crazy, even though his face moved with normal plasticity - he could smile and frown - unlike many Botoxed ladies he had seen whose visages were as frozen as the helmets of Medieval knights you saw in the museum.

The situation was certainly odd. How would he go anywhere - at least locally - that someone didn't know who he was? How would he face family and friends? He bent over and reached for his toes. The old flexibility was back as he touched the top of his shins and slid his finger ever lower. He also felt stronger than he had in a long time. Testing himself, he lifted twenty-five-pound free weights he had in his bedroom, and rarely used, straight up over his head. They felt remarkably light. Maybe he should order some thirty or forty pounders. Not really knowing what to do he pulled on some sweats and went for a jog, carefully keeping a towel over his head like Rocky Balboa so he would remain incognito. Who knew who would be driving by in the Hollywood Hills? It was commuter hour and someone could easily be coming along who recognized him. He covered the entire course he usually walked, from his house down to Franklin Avenue and up again all the way to Mulholland Drive, but this time mostly at a full run, jogging only at the steepest parts. He hadn't done that in years. When he arrived home, he came through the back door, dripping but exhilarated, his body pumped with endorphins. Something amazing was happening.

He was feeling so good that he decided to chance things and make an appearance at the club. Who knew - maybe he was wrong? Maybe the members would accept his new more youthful appearance or, more likely, simply ignore the transition. At worst he would have to deal with people gossiping behind his back. But that would be okay. He didn't have to listen, and after a certain amount of time, new subjects of interest, new scandals, would come up as they always do in human affairs. Of course, that would assume he didn't continue to get younger and soon look like a candidate for the college team. He took a last glance at himself in the mirror to reassure himself he still didn't look that young, just a healthy and vibrant fifty - the type that beamed out at him from the pages of Men's Health accompanying senior exercise programs or diet analyses for the aging male (more blueberries, please; easy on the ribeye). Nothing wrong with that.

So Dan Gelber went to his club, and walked straight to the front desk where Estrella, an older Filipina who was often stationed there, was ensconced, greeting members and making sure they signed for their guests so they were billed the requisite fee.

"Morning. Checking in," he said.

"Good morning," she replied, smiling at him "How do you do?" She scrutinized him for a moment, then broadened her smile. "You very much resemble a member here... Mr. Gelber. You look just like him. A son? Nephew?"

Gelber, at a loss replied. "No, I'm actually... myself."

"Welcome to Hancock Tennis Club then," she said, apparently unable or unwilling to process something so outlandish. "I hope you don't mind but..." Continuing pleasantly, she pushed the guest book toward him. "Please sign in."

"No, no, Estrella. ...*Soy yo, Dan Gelber. Cómo estás hoy?*" He said, speaking to her in Spanish as he occasionally did for practice. She stared at him, *"Es verdad. It's true. I'm Dan."* He pointed at himself for emphasis, just then noticing his image in the gilded mirror behind her beneath the club logo. He was astonished to see he looked younger still, maybe in his thirties. How was this possible?

At that point her lower jaw fairly flopped open and she uttered the word "What?" in a manner somewhere between a shocked scream and pharyngeal gasp. Then she clutched her stomach as if having heart attack.

Two busboys, who were scrubbing tables nearby, started running toward them, one of them shouting *"Llama al 911!"* as the other pulled out his phone.

"Are you okay?" said Gelber to Estrella who looked now as if she were about to vomit.

"Yes, I think so…. I…" she managed to say, looking up again and forcing a smile that could not hide her amazement. "I'm okay. I mean I'm okay."

"She's…okay," said Gelber, just barely relieved. He held up his hand for the busboys and started backing up while keeping his eye on Estrella. "It's just a surprise. She was… startled by me…"

Club members, including some he knew, hearing the commotion, were entering the lobby. Was that Amanda following behind them? That would have been too much. Before he could find out, Dan Gelber turned and bolted through the door.

IV
OPPORTUNITY

"I thought it was supposed to take several visits."

"In Ayurveda, each man and woman unique. All are different combination of three Doshas - Vatta, Pitta and Kapha."

"What am I?"

"More Vatta, than Pitta, but a little more Kapha than both. We will see."

"Great. Whatever that means. But, more importantly, I already look thirty-five or something. Am I going to be a teenager by the end of the week?"

"You no like being young?"

"I almost gave the lady at the front desk a heart attack. It's not so simple."

Gelber was pacing around Gombo's office. Extremely agitated, Dan had come there directly after the club, arriving unannounced, but the doctor was able to see him, almost as if he had anticipated Gelber's arrival. In fact, he was standing at the door waiting. And somehow Gelber knew that he would be there. He hadn't even bothered to call because of that. Somehow, he knew. It was the natural extension of where he was now. From Gelber's perspective, things had gotten so out of hand he no longer believed he was in control of his life. It seemed Gombo was. Still, he had to admit he felt good - at least physically. Better than he had in years. The bounce was back in his step. But was it his bounce?

"If you are happy as you are, stop taking tea. You will stay same, I think, not get younger, at least quickly. How many cups you have?"

"Nine now."

"So and so." Gombo weighed the possibilities. "How is prostate?"

"I'm pissing like a kid. Of course, the cancer could still be there. Probably is. I haven't been to the urologist."

"Is not there. Cancer is mental issue. Is spirit telling body is tired, does not wish to continue, so cells multiply."

"Sure." Gelber sounded less skeptical then he meant to, as if he actually believed Gombo. What was going on?

"You seem confused, Mr. Dan. This not big trouble. Consider possibility. Perhaps you would like to be twenty-two. That is great age. Start all over again." He smiled broadly. "Many new... how you say... horizons. Begin career another time. No mistakes. This time win Oscar. Write novel for Nobel Prize. Marry most beautiful woman in—"

"Please! Enough!" Gelber suddenly snapped, in spite of himself.

"Or don't marry. Have—"

"I can't take this anymore. Who're you, Mephistopheles, offering me to be twenty-two again? Did we make some kind of deal? When did that happen? You're going to take my soul in exchange for a second life?"

Gombo began to laugh. "Take soul? What would I do with it?"

"That's what you want, isn't it? I never made a deal with you. I just paid for a service. I should have known it was a trick when it was so cheap... Look, this is so crazy, I hardly know what I'm talking about and I certainly don't know what you're talking about, but this whole thing is mighty strange. I didn't come out to a half-empty shopping mall in Reseda to turn into some modern dress version of Faust - that's for sure. I just had a back ache. Okay a bad one, but still a back ache. If this is what's happening. I think I should just call it quits right here. Except that I... Except..." Gelber started anxiously touching his body, feeling the extra ripples that had appeared around his quadriceps, the new tautness to his hamstrings.

"Mr. Dan, Mr. Dan, Mr. Dan..." Gombo exhaled deliberately, more or less, Gelber thought, like a yoga instructor giving an illustration for an especially slow and recalcitrant student. He hated yoga classes and never attended them but that's how he envisioned it. "Sit down. Relax. No reason to upset yourself." He gestured to a chair. Reluctantly, Gelber complied, lowering himself onto the chair as if it might've been electrified or booby-trapped in some manner. "This Mephistopheles you speak of, this Faust... They taught it us when I went school Namche Bazaar. European literature class - three years. Balzac, Dickens, Tolstoy. Too many things we learned from West. Never learned our own things in that school. Perhaps because on way to Everest, many foreigners. Anyway, this is old story from German Goethe and some play writer from England... not Shakespeare."

"Marlowe."

"Yes. Even older story than that I am sure. Came from somewhere long ago. It is typical Western religious tradition, your folk tale like our Ramayana. Tut-tut-tut." Gombo wiggled his finger like a schoolmaster remonstrating students. Then he laughed. "That was my professor - from Brussels, Belgium. He gave warning by telling story of Faust. We never read. He just tell. Satan comes to man and gives temptation of wonderful deal. Man accepts, has good time for a while, does what he wants... girlfriends, money, famous, more girlfriends, more money... then Devil comes and takes man away, usually in fire, no?"

"Yes. These days maybe he'd die of radiation or global warming... Or from taking herbal medicines not approved by the FDA."

Gombo ignored the sarcasm and continued. "Good people get rewarded, bad people go to Underground for forever and ever. How stupid is that."

"What do you mean?"

"Mr. Dan, you intelligent man. You write books, movies."

"Did."

"Okay, did. Very good. So you know. That is not life. Just made up from Christian and Jewish bibles. God rewards good and punishes bad." He started to laugh yet again. "How silly is that - like a joke on human being. When did you ever see that? Maybe one, two times. In a movie or someone lucky. By accident. In life... in real life that everyone live... anything happen. Evil people die happy. Good people die sad with no money. Children get hit by car. Your religion promise to make all right in afterlife. What a trick. Is like form of torture. No one can enjoy self in present."

"Alright, alright, I'm not religious anyway," said Gelber, trying to cut off the lecture.

"I don't mean to insult, but Hindu religion much better, more true. We have many Gods. They do good things, bad things. All mixed up. Like life. Your religion made up to keep people unhappy. Guilty for everything they do."

This time Gelber exhaled. "Yeah, well…" How many times did he have to say he wasn't religious? "I guess you've got a point there. I can't remember a time I wasn't guilty - from about the age of four on, maybe two."

"Yes, I understand that is problem for Jewish people."

"No kidding."

The two men sat there for a while, before Gombo finally broke the silence. "Of course, you could have new life of fun."

"As a twenty-two-year-old freak who's really seventy-three?"

"What is wrong with that…? Of course, you would have to die first."

V

THE DREAMS OF KEW

That Dan Gelber found himself in Nepal seemed only the logical extension of everything that was happening to him. He never stopped to question it. He was on a high, trying to recapture something that, like many people, he may never have had. Still, it had all happened so quickly. On the flight over, he had put himself to sleep, reciting Kipling's couplet over and over, "The wildest dreams of Kew are the facts of Kathmandu," as if it were his personal version of "The quick brown fox jumped over the lazy dog." It made the interminable plane ride pass, if not quickly, at least tolerably. Good thing too. Never had he flown that long all in one gulp, nineteen hours in the air with barely forty minutes for the change in Bangkok. He was by himself. Gombo had gone ahead to make "arrangements," whatever that meant, leaving him in Los Angeles to sort out his departure, to inform those interested, a sufficient number for the purpose, all those he would normally call, some friends from the club and elsewhere, there weren't many anyway, that he was feeling miraculously better and had decided finally to live out a lifetime ambition by going trekking in Nepal.

Zack was surprised to hear from him so soon. "Two calls in week, pop? What's up?" When Dan told him, he was encouraging. "I can't believe you're feeling that good this quickly, but go for it, dude. Send pictures from the top of Everest."

"I don't think I'll go quite that far," Gelber responded. "I'm supposed to go to base camp, but if I make it to the tree line, I'll be lucky. Maybe some Sherpas will carry me. Or they'll strap me to a yak with a security blanket."

He forgot to ask about the kids again, he realized, after he hung up. Oh, well. Probably for the better under the circumstances.

Amanda was amazed. "It's the new you," she said when he called her to say good-bye. "I'm going to have to adjust." Then she dropped a bomb that would have put the kibosh on everything. "Hey, you know what? I know this sounds crazy but... Everest base camp? I wouldn't mind coming with you.... In fact, I'd love to. You're right - it's one of those lifetime things. Now or never."

He didn't say anything.

"Hey, cat got the old tongue-o. You're not planning on going with a group of Kama Sutra instructors or something? I won't put a crimp in your style, promise."

"No, no, no," Dan interjected, forcing a laugh while searching quickly for an excuse that would at least fly in the short run. "Nothing of the kind.... I could only wish... You're right though. It is kind of a new me... I was so near death... It's more of a... spiritual journey. I hope you don't mind, but maybe next time. I'll be your guide then. I really need to do it alone now, find my mantra and all that. If you meet the Buddha in the road, kill him, as they say."

"Oh, yes, definitely...Okay, I understand. I wouldn't want to get in the way of your enlightenment. Safe travels." She sounded skeptical, and a little defeated, but what could he do? He felt a bit sad. He admired Amanda's moxie. It was greater than his in its way. In another world he might have wanted her to come. But saying anything more would have made it worse, actually impossible. In the midst of the excitement of travel, especially to an exotic locale, Dan Gelber did not yet fully comprehend how determined he had already become for a second life, whatever the unintended consequences.

The approach to Kathmandu's Tribhuvan International Airport is unusually risky because of its unique geography set among the world's highest peaks. Despite the spectacular views the approach felt to Gelber more like an amusement park thrill ride, the kind that, at least for adults, one hopes will end as quickly as possible. Such things were for teenagers so far from death the whole idea of *rigor mortis* barely exists, let alone planes smashing into jagged rocks. This was not for middle-aged or older men bent on rejuvenation. So as Dan Gelber's plane came in for a landing, he was momentarily filled with dread—and not just because of the physical danger. Was he making a huge mistake? What was he doing here? If there ever were a fool's errand, this was it. He had no right to do this, he thought. It was against nature.

Caught in a down draft, the plane made a lurch to the left And bottomed out. For a split second, it did indeed look as if it were headed for an icy peak. Someone was shouting warnings into Gelber's earphones. "Get out! Get out! Everybody out!" How could he do that? "Go, go, go," it repeated. "Do not go back! Leave your belongings!" He heard a crackling noise and sirens, almost like a police car or a fire truck. Where was that coming from? He was in the air, not on the ground. Tensing, he sat up straight and involuntarily ripped off the earphones. But all was well as the plane skirted the peak and gently dipped onto terra firma, taxiing in with scarcely a bump.

The airport, Gelber noted as he loped, now feeling calmer and naturally jet lagged, into the terminal, the hub for Yeti Airlines, an outfit that serviced Siddharthanagar - translated as "Siddhartha Gautama's town," Buddhaville. He paused for a moment and took a deep breath, as if enacting a ritual. Perhaps he was headed for enlightenment, he mused, after all, though he knew very well he wasn't. It was something quite different and more selfish. The opposite, actually.

He was met at the baggage check by three short, extremely wiry men holding a sign with his name. He assumed them to be Sherpas, although they wore Western clothes. They waited until Gelber claimed his bag, a newly-purchased Patagonia backpack made of waterproof laminate and stuffed with gear one was supposed to bring on Himalayan treks, including La Sportiva super-gaiter mountaineering boots and multiple layers of North Face "responsibly sourced" 800 fill down parkas and fleeces rated for temperatures as low as forty below.

In "Paintbrush Red" the pack was easy to spot as it came down the conveyor. That was the intention, why it was chosen. Gelber waved off the men's help and slung it over his shoulder, following them to their car - an aging Range Rover that looked as if it had climbed up its share of mountains over the years. The tires had no visible tread. Stacked in the cargo were all manner of trekking equipment - tents, medical kit, cooking utensils. In the back seat was Gombo.

"Welcome to my country, Mr. Dan," he said, "I see you have met porters." He signaled for Gelber to get into the seat next to him. "From here we could take small plane to Lukla for base camp. But ride by car to Jiri better for our purpose."

"Sounds good" Gelber said, slumping down in the seat exhausted. He had had enough of planes and mountains. Moments later they were whirling past the sites of Kathmandu with its Buddhist and Hindu temples guarded by armies of monkeys. Out of the corners of his bleary eyes, Gelber noticed tourists and locals, mingling with monks in orange robes and aging hippies who seemed to have been transported to Nepal directly from the Summer of Love.

Soon they were out on the open highway, local version, twisting and turning along the narrowest of roads between stratospheric peaks the likes of which Gelber had never seen, but that Gombo assured him were as yet only foothills. They were held up for an hour when a bus, decorated with a beaded elephant head, was stalled with its back wheels in a pothole. By the time the way was clear, Dan had fallen asleep. When he awoke who knew how much later, they were approaching their destination, the tiny Everest gateway town of Jiri. They spent the night there in a small hotel and woke up early the next morning to begin the trek to the base camp, the same route, Gombo explained, as the one taken by Tensing Norgay and Edmund Hillary when they were the first to reach the summit of the world's highest mountain, the one known locally as Sagarmatha.

Gelber was surprised how easily he was able to handle the first part of the trek. They started at only six thousand feet, so the altitude did not affect him seriously. Besides, one of the porters was carrying his new bright red pack on his front while attaching tents and other gear to his back. That was how it was done, a remnant of the white man's burden era. Gelber could live with it. For once he did not feel guilty. Perhaps it was the Buddhist environment, he thought, no judgment, as they passed a small stupa of stacked stones by the trail. They were climbing slowly through a grove of rhododendron as tall as pine trees, petals falling from their brilliant pink flowers to carpet the way as rhesus monkeys swung from the branches. It was almost Disney-like. Soon the foliage gave way, however, as they approached the timber line. The trail grew steeper, stone stairs, seemingly centuries old, cut into the sharper inclines. Tiny Sherpa women, belongings piled improbably on their heads, raced past them on bare feet.

Gelber and the porters proceeded on as one of the true Himalayan peaks finally appeared before them, not Everest but Cho Oyu, itself over 27,000 feet and one of the highest in the world. Before it was a giant gorge that looked several thousand feet deep with raging rapids running at the bottom. A rope bridge ran across it, swaying back and forth with a bottom of flimsy-looking wood planks that seemed made for someone to fall through, barely able to catch hold as they plummeted to their death. At first Gelber was scared to cross, frozen in place watching the Sherpa women skittering to the other side where a tea house stood, their destination for the night.

Gombo and the porters smiled, recognizing his fear. "Tomorrow you will not have to cross more," said Gombo. Gelber nodded. He understood. The new Dan was coming. Holding a deep breath and not daring to look down or to the sides, he made his way across.

That night, he sat with Gombo in the small dining room/kitchen of the tea house eating curry and rice and taking a few tokes on a hash pipe.

"Why did you ever leave here? Your country is incredibly beautiful."

"Beautiful, yes. But sometimes I prefer other. Bad karma to stay in one place. Can be dangerous for next life." Dan waited for him to elucidate but Gombo didn't seem to want to continue. He said something to the woman who was cooking. She brought a kettle with boiling water, pouring a cup for Gelber. Gombo took an envelope and emptied the contents into the cup.

"My tea? Is it the same as before?"

"Perhaps little stronger. You will need for... fresh start." He studied Gelber a moment. "You could still say no, Mr. Dan. But would be shame..."

"After coming all this way?"

"Is long journey I know. But you see Cho Oyu. Tomorrow you see Sagamartha."

"Everest... What does that mean in Nepalese?"

"Forehead of Sky."

Nice, Gelber thought, then stared down at the cup, frowning and wondering if he was really going to drink it.

"Everyone will love you in new life, Mr. Dan. You will write beautiful things. Better than before. As good as writers Belgian teach. Maybe better. You will know so much from beginning."

Gelber looked up. "No, not a second time. All those hours alone in a room. Never again." Gombo raised his eyebrows ever so slightly. Gelber smiled at his curiosity. "'It's lousy to write but great to have written.'"

"Ah, very clever." Gombo smiled too. "You are good writer."

"I wish it was me but it's Dorothy Parker."

"Who is that?"

"Lady from the 1920s. Liked martinis. Anyway, I don't want to write. Too much sitting. I'll get a bad back all over again. I want to do something active, if I'm to start over. Something completely different. Something that would really make me happy this time."

"What is?"

"I think I know. Do I have to tell you?"

"No, why?"

Gelber stared again at the tea. "How big will I be if I drink this stuff?"

"How big you want?"

"Oh, like six-two, six-three… That's pretty much the best for what I'm thinking of."

"How tall you now?"

"Five-seven."

Gombo broke into one of his horse laughs. "Ha-ha, we stretch you out then…. But be careful. Always take. Otherwise go backward. Maybe you shrink and hair fall out. Floor look like barber shop." He laughed at that one too. But then he reached into a sack and sprinkled some yellowish powder into the mix. "We give you special extra one time. Shoot you up like beanstalk Jack. Not too much though. Otherwise you giant and scare people."

"You sure I don't have to make a deal with you? There's no quid pro quod? No contract?"

"Contract in Himalaya? All contract in Himalaya with Shiva himself. No one else. Well, maybe Kali. She get angry some time if you forget her. But you don't need."

"What happens if I run out of tea?"

"I give you pill too. Same thing."

"And if I run out of them?"

"You come see me."

"At the mini-mall…"

"As long as they not raise rent… But no worry. If problem, I find you."

"How're you going to do that?"

"How I make you look like kid again? Turn broken back old man into Mr. Charles Atlas at the Center of Rockefeller."

"I still don't know why you're doing this."

"Perhaps is what you call pro bono." Gombo spoke the last words with mock solemnity, then broke into yet another of his laughs but stopped abruptly this time. "You still guilty? Nothing good come without pain or punishment? What is matter, Mr. Dan? How you say - you look gift horse in mouth? Everyone know Western man don't believe in God now, so why you worry?"

Gelber was about to say "good point," but he realized he had said substantially the same thing before for the same reason. It was an argument hard to dispute.

"Have second thought is okay," said Gombo.

"No. no…. No second thoughts."

Gelber sat there a last moment before drinking the tea. Then, before he could change his mind, lifted the cup and gulped it down in one swallow without even holding his nose. Surprisingly, it didn't taste bad, but was remarkably smooth, almost like an ordinary cup of jasmine or oolong.

The next morning he arose early and followed the porters and Gombo down another yet narrower trail along the gorge. They carried his pack and equipment as they normally did, although he felt as if he could carry just about anything, while he took pictures with his cell phone. He was feeling remarkably strong, ready to break his record for deadlifts if he were near a gym. It even seemed, although perhaps he was imagining, that he had already grown an inch or so. Was the tea working already? It was hard to believe, astonishing actually, but Dan Gelber had to acknowledge there was a quickness to his step he could not remember having even at the age of twenty, or ever for that matter. They passed through a crevasse and for a moment the trail almost seemed to disappear, but then popped up again in a few hundred feet. After roughly half a mile, they rounded a curve suddenly to see a sharp peak looming behind another somewhat smaller but still gigantic mountain. Gelber recognized this peak instantly from myriad photographs and films — Sagamartha, "The Forehead of the Sky." He had childhood memories from the documentary of Hillary and Norgay standing at the top. He took some pictures himself, before they continued around the bend another hundred yards or so where yet another rope bridge, this one more threadbare and likely not highly trafficked, crossed the gorge.

"We have arrived," said Gombo, looking around carefully as if to satisfy himself they were alone. No one was near. He nodded to one of the porters who pulled a nearly machete-sized knife from a wooden sheaf, walked over to the bridge and hacked at the point the rope was tied to a lead hook cemented to a rock. He cut through it with two mighty swings, sending the entire bridge plunging into the gorge. Seconds thereafter another porter hurled Gelber's brand new Patagonia backpack after it. They all watched as the laminated pack bounced off the sides of the gorge, landing in the rapids below, a bright red object no one could miss bobbing in and out of the water as it headed toward the flatlands and civilization.

"You are dead now, Mr. Dan." said Gombo "So sad story - trying to reach Everest base camp. Foolish thing for man your age. A pity so many try climb when should know better." He shook his head, then looked back at Gelber, pointing to yet another trail that wound behind a granite outcropping. "Now you start over…. No one recognize you… Eyes new color… hair new color… Go! … Go!"

Those words again. Go, go. They kept repeating, as if it weren't just Gombo speaking them, as if someone else were saying them now, urging people to get out. But from where? They were alone on the mountain. He thought he heard a siren and the crackling sound again, growing in intensity as it had on the plane. Then, gradually, it subsided.

Everything was silent, as if time had been frozen, allowing space for a narrative to flow non-stop through his brain in the manner, he imagined, one's life was supposed to unroll in front of you at the moment of death – thought instant to thought instant, Heaven to Hell, as the Zensters say.

Dan hesitated another moment, glancing over at Gombo who nodded to him pleasantly.

Then he sprinted for the trail… to a new life.

VI
FUTURES

He had set the ball machine only slightly faster than he used to, but the balls seemed to be coming with higher velocity than he expected - first right, then left, then center. Even with his new body or whatever it was, he struggled to hit them. Most were deep in the court or skidding off the line, the way you were supposed to hit to push your opponent back to set yourself up to win the point. But this time the machine was doing it to him. Perhaps it was because he was indoors where the surfaces were unusually fast and the lighting insufficient. Still, he didn't like the excuse. He would try again.

He corralled the balls with the sweeper and filled the machine, then walked back to the receiving side without adjusting anything downwards, not giving himself that excuse, before pressing the remote. The balls came just as fast. He missed the first one or two again, but suddenly something clicked in. He was hitting them, cross court, down the line at an imaginary someone's back hand, straight at the machine to handcuff them, just as he had seen Nadal and Djokovic do on the Tennis Channel. Set up the point and move in to dictate. Feeling cocky, he did just that, taking a ball on the fly midcourt and surprising himself by returning it deftly into the corner.

"Not bad," a voice said. "Can you do it twice in a row?"

He turned to see a black man wearing traditional tennis whites sitting in one of those moveable electric chairs used by the disabled. The man pressed a button with a shriveled hand and motored forward.

"If you can't repeat again and again, you never did it," the man said. "It doesn't count."

"Thanks for the vote of confidence."

"I'm not being mean. I'm just telling you the truth, young fella."

He tightened involuntarily. Being called "young fella" still startled him. Sure he had had the expression aimed at him before, but, until recently, for the last thirty years or so, it was meant sarcastically. Now it was for real.

"When I coached Roddick, I made him hit the same shot four hundred times in a row."

"You coached Roddick?"

"For a while. He couldn't take the discipline. Look what happened to him. One major and out. Flash in the pan."

"What's your name?"

"Derek Hicks…. And you're?"

"Uh… Jay Reynolds." For a split second, he almost forgot. It was new after all, roughly six weeks.

"Well, Jay, nice meeting you," said Hicks, reaching down again to turn his chair around and leave, then waving good-bye with the shriveled left hand that looked as if it had been mashed up in a washing machine or a garbage disposal.

"Roddick was the last great American hope."

Hicks hesitated. Slowly he turned back. "Yes, he was. He won the US Open way back in oh-three. Since then, no Yanks. No Sampras, no Agassi, no Johnny Mac. The glory days are over for our country. Will they ever come back?" He broke into a wide grin. "Perhaps Jay Reynolds can do it. Got a ways to go though. Keep practicing. Get out front of that backhand more. Everything on the rise." He spun around a second time and disappeared behind the tarpaulin that hung behind the court.

It took Jay a few moments to get back to the machine again. Hicks was the first person he had exchanged more than a few words with since he had been back. He had decided to hide out for a while, get used to his new identity, and had come up to this island off Seattle where he knew they had indoor courts so he could begin his training in private. He was surprised to find someone like Hicks there. That night he looked up the disabled man on the Internet. He found Hicks was forty-six and at the age of twenty-four had been a ranking player - number sixty-seven in the world, which was not bad, and headed upwards - when his Jetta was side-swiped by a semi on the way to play in the Cincinnati Open. Hicks spent eleven months in the ICU before he even got to rehab. And another several years before he became a coach in a motorized chair.

Jay—or was it Dan—wondered if it was serendipity and this was the coach for him. But it was too early for that. He hadn't fully shed his old identity, wasn't, for that matter, sure that he would ever be able to do it. The confusion would be too much.

Indeed the first few weeks after departing Gombo, heading off down the trail and eventually making his way back to Kathmandu on a rickety bus he thought would go over a cliff about a dozen times en route, ending his second life before it barely began, Dan Gelber was having a distinct problem knowing who he was. He had in his pocket the address of a man Gombo told him was a former leader of a defunct Maoist rebellion against the Nepalese crown now a figure in their underworld. He would be able to provide Dan with papers for his new identity, a US passport Gombo assumed would pass muster. Gelber, however, would have to provide that identity, choose one that would function for his new purposes. For various reasons, that wouldn't be easy. And without that identity, obviously, he could not begin his new life. In that regard, Gombo had left him in the lurch, although the Reseda shaman had never promised more. Dan would have to forge a second self by himself. "It is better for all doshas," Gombo had said.

He spent the next few weeks trying to figure this out, while moving from one guest house to another in the bohemian Thamel district, never staying too long in one because he was growing so quickly, as much as two inches in one week, that it might raise suspicions. It was enough he as yet had no passport and had to effectively bribe his way into the houses, surreptitiously dropping three or four times the number of rupees required for a room on the host's counter. Gelber had more than enough cash with him for the purpose, secreted in a zipped leather pouch, and yet more - his life savings in fact— transferred with surprising ease to a numbered account in the Caymans before he left.

Meanwhile, he continued his extraordinary growth spurt, feeling at once unnerved and exhilarated. Soon he found himself bumping his head on the low doorways of the ancient buildings. He had to learn to adjust, to bend over, something that he had rarely done at five- seven. The beds were becoming too small for him too. He would pull off the bedding and sleep on the floor. Several times he woke up in the small hours of the morning with an oddly familiar— yet somehow distant—ache in his knees. Then he realized they were growing pains, what he and most of his friends experienced when they were back in junior high or grammar school. How strange for that to be happening now as an adult, even one getting progressively younger. He grew muscles he had never felt in years, perhaps never had in the first place. He could jump and run faster than he ever imagined. He discovered he could do chin-ups, a lot of them, push-ups with one hand. One morning he got up and did a hundred burpees without stopping. His hair color too was changing, becoming lighter as if he had been spending all his days in the sun playing tennis or swimming. But he hadn't. He had been doing something quite different. He had been passing most of the daylight hours in coffee shops—moving from one to another for the same reason he changed guest houses—using their wifi connections to scan the internet for possibilities for his new identity.

Dan Gelber knew that if he became a famous tennis star the press would look into his family history. What background would have the best chance of being undetected, of not raising questions? Such a thing would be difficult to find. But if he didn't there would be no point in going forward. Gelber had often speculated about the results of fame in his life, often obsessively, but this time he was confronting it in a new way. It was a real possibility.

He would conduct this research while drinking endless cups of tea, both the coffee shop's and Gombo's. Sometimes in the process—it was tedious— his mind would drift off, wondering what people were thinking back home. Had his disappearance been noted as yet? Did someone pick up the Patagonia backpack and discover his passport inside? Was the inevitable conclusion drawn? What did Zack tell his children? What was Amanda thinking? These were uncomfortable thoughts and Dan Gelber tried to push them away. What did he matter to these people anyway, he thought. They had their lives to live. He should have his—a second one. What harm would that be? Out of sight, out of mind, as the hoary expression went. The old Dan would soon be forgotten, as would most people who had not made an indelible mark on their times.

One time he even found himself wondering about his ex-wife Cynthia. Had she heard of his disappearance? Should he have told her of his departure, even though they had been divorced for decades? Just to say good-bye. But Gelber did his best to dismiss the thought. Zack undoubtedly did and, besides, Cynthia had a new life of her own and was remarried to an anthropology professor and living in Philadelphia.

It was in the midst of that cogitation he discovered what he had been searching for. He had been scanning obituaries for the state of Tennessee for 2002. He had also been surveying Texas and Oklahoma for the same year. It would have only been three after the new Dan would have been born and in a location sufficiently far from California in order not to arouse suspicion. What had drawn Dan's attention was a couple—Martin and Dorothea Reynolds—that had died in a fire in a trailer park in Smyrna, a suburb of Nashville. The short obit told the story of the pair who, serendipitously for Gelber, were both orphans and had met in an orphanage as children. In other words, had no known parents or family of any kind. Dan searched their names further on the internet and found nothing. No mention of them as a couple whatever. This was what he was indeed looking for. Why couldn't they have had a son, he posited? The young boy could have been lost in the shuffle, simply overlooked by the press. Who would remember now after so many years? Moreover, Dan Gelber knew the Nashville area, more or less, having spent time there on location for a movie of the week he had written some years ago. At least he knew it enough to pass, should anyone ask questions.

Within the hour Gelber was at the address Gombo had given him. It turned out to be a warehouse in an industrial suburb of the city. A video camera peered down at him from above the door which had a discreet set of Chinese characters above it. Dan pressed the doorbell and was buzzed in immediately. Inside was a surprisingly high-tech installation with numerous computers and printers, some 3-D, all apparently Chinese made. But of course, they were near Tibet and China had control of that country and, by extension, great influence in Nepal.

A man in a blue smock approached. "Nawang Gombo," he said. Gelber nodded. He was clearly expected. "Two thousand five hundred US dollars," the man continued.

Dan reached into his money belt and counted out the money.

"What name?"

"Jay Reynolds," he said. It had come to him almost in a flash—the errant son of Martin and Dorothea. But the more Dan Gelber thought of it, the more he liked it. It would sound good on the lips of an announcer or in the headlines of a newspaper. He could see it now on the sports pages of the Los Angeles Times and the New York Times or maybe as the subject of an in-depth study in The New Yorker replete with a free-hand drawing of his new profile, an American resurgence, out of the middle border, as they said, direct from Smyrna, Tennessee. Jay Reynolds - what more middle American name could a Jewish boy ever wish for?

Gelber heard it again several weeks later when he encountered Derek Hicks for a second time. "Hey, Reynolds, looking good. More or less. Where'd you get that one-handed backhand? Pretty old school." Dan was bent over the water cooler. He had been hitting with a guy from the University of Washington team. Hicks - who evidently had been watching - was holding the tarpaulin open with the side of his wheelchair.

"Just getting ready for my first Futures tournament." said Dan - or was it Jay - looking up from the cooler.

"Really? That's ambitious. Hope you're prepared to get your ass kicked. Pro's a whole different ballgame from the college team."

"I was never on the college team."

"Really? You seem like a college boy…. Freshman or maybe a sophomore. Anyway, good luck. And if your legs feel heavy, remember - it's nerves." Hicks started to exit, spinning around in his chair.

"Wait, wait…" He took some steps toward Hicks who hesitated. "I was thinking… I… um…. I'm gonna need a coach."

"For the Futures? No one uses a coach for them, unless it's his mother. Maximum money's fifteen hundred and there's only one winner."

"I'm thinking long term. I'll pay. Wanna do it?"

"What is this 'white skin privilege'?' You exploiting black people, boy?" Jay was about to take umbrage when he noticed the grin on Hicks's face. "Don't worry. I'm married to one." He stopped and wheeled up to Jay, looking him straight in the eye. "Now let me ask you a serious question. Why the fuck do you want to do this? Over a billion people in the world play or watch tennis, almost as many as soccer and basketball and hoity-toity cricket. And those are team sports. Tennis is solo. It's as competitive as all get out and you gotta be fitter than a boxer and as smart as a chess player. Your chances of making a decent living at it are about as good as being the first man on Alpha Centauri."

"I want to try."

"Try?… Is that all?…. I've seen your kind before. You think if you can hit a halfway decent overhead, you're going to have Roger Federer's endorsements and spend the rest of your life in Maria Sharapova's underpants. You should be going to college and studying something useful. I saw you playing with that kid from U. of Washington."

"I told you - I'm not in college. Did that a long time ago. Two Ivy League degrees and they were worth nothing."

"What?!"

"Just kidding."

"How old are you?" Hicks was getting impatient.

"Born February 11, 1999." Jay recited the full date of birth from the passport to remind himself. "Twenty last month. Still plenty of time."

"For what?"

"To make it big."

"Nadal and Sampras already won Roland Garros and the US Open by the time they were nineteen and you're just starting to play in some rinky-dinky Futures against high school kids and their pot-bellied uncles with pacemakers under their Lacostes... Where is this tournament for the ages?"

"Laguna Niguel."

"Laguna bloody balls two-bit Niguel, down there near San Juan Capistrano and all the swallows. I played there once. The courts had so many cracks you thought you were charging net over an earthquake fault... Have you got your IPIN yet?"

"What's that?"

"Oh, man. Have I got a doozy here." He started wheeling away again, half muttering to himself. "Doesn't know what an IPIN is and expects to play Futures tennis. Now I believe you. You didn't go to college."

Jay followed after.

An IPIN, it turned out, was a personal identification number from the International Tennis Foundation and cost all of sixty bucks. But without it you couldn't play Futures tournaments and therefore couldn't get the ranking points necessary to lift you into more serious competition. Hicks filled him in on the details when they sat in the club refreshment area.

"I hope you're ordering the smoothie with the chia seeds."

"Chia seeds? You sound like Gom...." Dan stopped himself.

"Gum? I'm talking about chia seeds. Got something against chia? They give you energy. You can use it on the court. They say the Aztecs ate them before they went into battle."

"That's not all they ate. They boiled water to eat the conquistadors before they could get to Tenochtitlan."

"Tenochtitlan?" Hicks eyed him curiously. "Where'd you learn that?"

"High school."

"Most kids in high school these days barely know who Abraham Lincoln was."

"I went to a good school... Look, I would love it if you would come with me. I need a coach. I may know about the Aztecs, read a book about them once, but I don't know fuck all about Futures tournaments. You've been there before. I'm serious about this stuff. I want to win. I want to go all the way."

Hicks stared at him. "Where was that high school?"

"Tennessee."

"Like Ernie Ford...."

"And Johnny Cash. Look, just come with me once and if it doesn't work out..."

"They won't let me coach you while you're playing - you know that. Only the women are allowed to do that."

"Yeah, I know. I saw it on television."

"Of course, in the Futures nobody really cares..... Are you honest?"

"What?"

"You heard me - are you honest? Do you cheat? Because I won't coach anyone who isn't honest. I made some mistakes before and I don't want to go through that again. .... Can you resist temptation?"

"What is this - Sunday school? I don't cheat. In fact, you can't cheat. There's GPS calling the lines."

"Not at the lower levels. And there's all kinds of stuff going on, my friend. Players on steroids and God knows what, gamblers paying them to tank matches, even games and points. Unless they're somebody's mother, half the crowd is punching bets on their cell phones or calling their bookies."

"Okay, okay. No, I'm not corrupt and I'm not dishonest," Dan said, feeling an unpleasant twinge and pushing it away. "And I don't even know any bookies... Mr. Hicks... Derek ... I'll do you proud. I'll... make up for Roddick. I'll practice like hell. I'm in it for the glory of the game. I'm not interested in money.... I have plenty of that."

"An heir. Lucky you."

"Not that. I made it all myself... even though I'm young."

"A prodigy then.... Were you a country singer back in Nashville?"

"No, no. I was just kidding."

"You do a lot of that, young man."

"Yeah. I guess I do... Just trying to keep things straight... It's difficult sometimes, but I'm working on it... Anyway, I can scrape together enough to pay you to get started.... And then who knows?"

Hicks sat on the side in Laguna Niguel, his wheelchair positioned at the end of the row. The courts had improved, he acknowledged, since he had played there himself. It was a sleek tennis club now, suitable for its Orange County location. No cracks visible and, as was conventional now, the court had just the right amount of grit added to the concrete, making it play almost, but not quite, like red clay. The balls jumped up with top spin. The intention these days - stated or otherwise - was to unify the playing speed on all tournament courts across the world as much as possible, equalizing clay and hard and ending the era of the specific court specialist. The US Open, Roland Garros, the Australian Open, even Wimbledon, although on grass and therefore a special case, were now relatively the same in how they played. It was part of the big business globalization of the game and some complained about it. But in the end, it made it easier for the players who were on a tough schedule in the first place. Some regularity was the object.

And that day in Laguna Niguel was a perfect day for tennis - in the low seventies and slightly overcast, making it easier as well to keep the sun out of your eyes on the serve and overhead. Nature was doing its work for the competitors and their few fans.

Stretching out, Dan felt optimistic. Only in the Futures could absolutely anyone play in the qualifying rounds. All you had to do was get that IPIN and sign up. And in Laguna it sure looked that way. There were some gangly kids who kept over hitting balls to show how strong they were and ended up flying them into the next court and some older guys who looked as if they were trying to recapture their glory days on the college team, if they were ever even on it. Dan's first opponent appeared to be one of the latter, a 42-year old in a sleeveless Arizona State sweatshirt with a gut hanging about six inches over his belt. The guy was already gasping for air in the warm-ups. Dan deliberately moved him back and forth to exploit the situation. This was going to be the proverbial piece of cake. But then, when official play started, the guy won the first set handily 6-2.

"Shit on a stick!" Dan said, slamming his racket into the fence a few yards from Hicks and nearly breaking it the way he did in high school when losing for the JV team.

"Watch it. You only have two and you don't want to have to borrow a racket. And by the way, you're the first person I've heard say shit on a stick in twenty years. Your father teach you?"

"Grandfather... I should be murdering that guy." He gestured back over the net.

"Yes, you should."

"Look, I'm sorry I brought you down here. This is all a mistake. I'm not cut out for professional sports. I blow under pressure. Let's forget it ever happened."

"What was your strategy?"

"What?"

"Your strategy! Surely you know what a strategy is. S... t...."

"Yes, your majesty! I know what strategy is. And it was obvious. Guy had a dinky sliced backhand and I kept playing it."

"Weak backhand, eh?" He shook his head as if Dan were a subnormal.

"Right."

"Then you play the forehand."

Dan flushed with embarrassment. Of course, he thought. Through strength to weakness. He had learned that long ago. How could he have been so stupid?

"You obviously knew that," said Hicks, reading Dan's mind. It wasn't difficult under the circumstances. "But playing in tournaments is totally different. Tension freezes the mind... and the body follows after. You have to learn everything all over again. Especially things you thought you knew well."

"Hey, we playin'?" came a voice from across the court.

"Strength to weakness. Keep moving your legs before the service return. And stay inside the baseline. Don't be static. Attack."

"Yes, yes. Be right there!" Dan yelled.

He won the next two sets 6-1, 6-2.

He also won the tournament, playing better each round and better than he ever had in the finals. It was if he were a man possessed - and maybe he was. Every shot he conceived, every idea he had, landed in. He was painting the lines in both corners with his forehand and backhand, structuring points at will, serving down the T with uncanny accuracy. If tennis was, as the late Robin Williams once cracked, chess at ninety miles an hour, Dan (or rather Jay) was a budding grand master. His opponent - an up-and-comer too who had already made the finals in three previous Futures and had once even made it to the third round in a Challengers tournament, the next rung up that often had several top professionals in the draw - couldn't believe it.

"I don't recognize you from the tour," he said to Dan as he trotted to the net for the congratulatory handshake. "Where'd you come from?"

"Kathmandu."

The man laughed.

Before the trophy ceremony, Dan ran over to where Hicks was sitting in his chair to thank him. Standing next to him was a young woman Dan had never seen before. She had ringlets of rust colored hair cascading down against the palest of caramel skin and the bluest of blue eyes, giving her the traditional appearance of a Louisa May Alcott character, yet completely modern. Dan experienced something he hadn't in decades. He immediately wanted to marry her. Have a baby. Buy a house. Pick out which preschool would be the least atrocious. It was a bourgeois fiesta in less than ten seconds. But people these days didn't get married until they were well into their thirties. What was he thinking?

"This is my daughter Molly," said Hicks.

"Hi, Jay," said Molly. "Congratulations on the win. You looked terrific out there."

"It wasn't me. Your father rescued me. He's a phenomenal coach."

"He is. The best. You're very lucky." She smiled at Dan who, inexplicably, almost blushed.

"He didn't tell me he had a daughter."

"Easy, Reynolds. She's too old for you…. Molly's twenty-five… in her third year of med school already. "

"Sure. Yes… too old."

"Going to be an orthopedist and take care of her father's rotting bones. She thinks she can cure me and get me walking again, so I can take you on. And don't think I won't. You're still a long way off….. So don't get cocky. You have no idea what's ahead of you. The advice I gave you was for beginners and your body isn't nearly ready for serious competition. If you hadn't won this rinky-dink tournament, I would have dropped you cold."

Back in the Himalayas, Dan Gelber had asked Gombo whether he would forget the past.

"Do you want to, my friend?" said the shaman. "Sometimes it will be useful to you, sometimes not. It is for you to decide if you want to remember. It is an act of will."

For much of the time, Dan surprised himself by blocking out the past - or simply not remembering. Those memories, he knew, were inconsistent with a second life. They would have a way of interfering with the future, of undermining new goals. But try as he might, from time to time, and mostly late at night, the doom and gloom of human existence, the ruptures that occur in everybody's life, came back to haunt him. Sometimes, even though it happened so long ago, he would dwell on how he and Cynthia had both betrayed each other, ending in an acrimonious divorce that left then five-year old Zack shuttling between cities and homes. The boy had school problems for years, despite his parents being honor students. Were those being recapitulated by Peter, carried out by yet another generation? Dan Gelber would rationalize this sad history, push it away, by choosing to blame his behavior, his and wife's, on the zeitgeist of the 1970s. They had married young and everyone else was out having fun. Why not them? It was the era of open marriage and self-fulfillment. Actualize the self was the mantra. And if that meant lying to yourself and others, it didn't matter. It would all be fine in the end because everyone would get what they wanted. Or, as Mick Jagger famously wrote, what they needed.

Well, that was then and this was now and now meant getting up every morning at 6:30 to a breakfast of oatmeal and bananas, sometimes with berries or a sprinkling of walnuts. This was followed by a five-mile run, usually up and down the hills of his Puget Sound island, then came time on the court - one hundred balls to the forehand, one hundred to the backhand, one hundred volleys. One shot missed, he started over, counting from one. The lunch that came next - most often fruit and grilled chicken, occasionally a small portion of pasta - was a welcome respite that didn't last long. By one he was back on the court for match play, playing two out of three or even three out of five, the loser to drop down for pushups or sent out for another run. This bought him to 4PM - the gym. That meant a round of weights, emphasizing the core and lower body especially, planks of every conceivable variety and endless monster walks with the red band, then squats and deadlifts. He was already at 310 pounds on the deadlifts and pushing upwards, but this was nothing, Hicks said. He hadn't found the right trainer for Dan yet. Nadal, Federer, Djokovic - those guys were machines. They could work out until the cows came home, went and came back again. The young guns coming up—Tsitsipas and Zverev— were doing similar regimens. If he couldn't train that way, there was no hope for him. He would fade faster than Roddick. And Roddick, Hicks told him, could deadlift 420.

Dan worked hard and soon he was in better shape than he could ever remember having been in, even when his original persona was twenty and the layers of fat had yet to appear. He certainly didn't have them now. He was a lean machine with the first inklings of a six-pack beginning to stripe his abdomen.

Sometimes he felt like Rocky Balboa. Sometimes he felt like a wreck. Whatever the case, he slept well. He'd hit the pillow at nine, try to read a book and be gone before he knew it. He dreamed as never before, mostly of Molly, of them locked in an embrace or, on a couple of occasions, marching down the aisle together. How could this have happened so quickly, Dan Gelber wondered? Why directly to nuptials? Why not just, you know, some hot sex and let it go at that, he thought? He was more of a romantic than he thought he was, or more traditional, more programmed than even he realized. He was of his generation, not hers. Hook-ups did not appeal, although, on second or third thought, or dream, he told himself he might get used to them. Not that he had any idea if she did hook-ups, or much idea of her at all for that matter. It was as if she had been placed before him by some divine force, an image of perfected young woman—his coach's own daughter— on which to project whatever he wanted.

One of those dreams came to him as a warning, however. They were at a club, dancing, when Dan said to her of the band, "They sound like 'The Animals." "What animal?" "No, no. *The* Animals. You know - Eric Burdon... 'House of the Rising Sun'... 'There is a house in New Orleans...'" He sang the phrase. Molly stared at him blankly and when it suddenly dawned on Dan he was referring to a song recorded fifty years ago. He might as well have been talking about John Phillip Sousa for all it meant to her. And they didn't have to learn that in school or sing it at football games. "Forget it," he said. "I mixed something up." He woke up thinking it was not just sixties rock, but a whole list of things, decades of emotional and intellectual detritus, opinions about everything under the sun, a good number of which that shining orb had already set on. But they were still the fabric of his former life. He wondered if Molly had even heard of "La Dolce Vita" and

"Jules and Jim," the films that had propelled him to want to write movies when he was barely out of high school. Or Bergman's "Wild Strawberries." How could he have a relationship with her if he had to censor everything he said, not that they had a relationship, but still... Damn, Gombo! Why did he let this part slide? Why wasn't memory erased? But without memory he would have no pleasure in his second life, would he, nothing to overcome, no final victory, on the court or off, when you couldn't remember what you were triumphing over in the first place.

Not that the triumphs were easy to come by. The step up from Futures tournaments to the Challengers proved to be more difficult than expected. He did okay in the Northbay Healthcare Men's Pro Championship in Fairfield, California, making it to the third round, but didn't get out of the qualifiers at the Las Vegas Tennis Open, losing in straight sets to a seventeen-year old kid from Belarus who was playing in his first American tournament. That he was six foot seven and served at 138 MPH might have been an excuse, but the kid was ranked 1698 out of about 1800 in the world on the ATP website. Dan hadn't even cracked the list.

"You know why that teenager beat you?" Hicks said. "He comes from a poor country. It's their only way out. That's why all those Eastern Europeans are dominating. You're a rich American boy. You don't need it."

"I need it. I just double-faulted in the tie-breaker."

"You shouldn't have been in a tie-breaker. Then you just folded up and lost the second set 6-1." He shrugged his shoulders and exhaled. He seemed more disappointed than Dan, almost dejected for a moment.

"Sorry about that."

"Maybe we moved you up too fast. But if you can't get out of the Futures, the whole thing's an exercise in futility.... I don't know. The competitive thing's probably not for you. It's not for everybody. They've got a father buried in their brain somewhere they don't want to overthrow or something. Don't know if that's you. I see you're testy sometimes and say weird things, but deep down... not on the surface, mind you... you're too nice a guy to win. You don't want to kill."

"There's next week in Cali, Colombia," Dan said, trying with only middling success to sound optimistic.

"Forget that. The Argentinian Davis Cup team's all over the draw and it's on dirt. You've been on hard courts the whole time. It's a recipe for disaster. You gotta build confidence."

"I can practice on clay for a few days. Anyway I..." He stopped. He was going to say he first learned to play tennis on clay with his father and uncles when he was six. But that was in the Bronx in the 1950s.

Hicks was staring at him. "Anyway what?"

"Forget it."

"Look, Reynolds, go to Cali, if you want to, but I won't be there. It's Linda and my twenty-fifth anniversary and we're having a party at the country club on the island. We'd be pleased to have you, if you would like to come."

He smiled at Dan as if to forgive him for his bad tennis. But he didn't need forgiveness. Molly would be there. "I'd be honored to come," he said.

"Glad to hear it. Sorry I snapped at you. I was upset with myself more than anything else. Not everyone has to be a great tennis player. Life is about other things."

That night, the Las Vegas tournament wrapped up, at least for him, Dan stood along the faux-canal of The Venetian Hotel watching the faux-gondolas stream by with their not-faux tourists. Off in the distance, a soprano sang an aria from *La Traviata* surprisingly well. Dan had grown to like Vegas over the years, when he had been alive in his previous life, not for the gambling or even for the ersatz absurdity of it all, but for the food. You could get a better meal in Sin City than just about anywhere on the planet. Maybe it was all those Chinese high rollers bringing in their own chefs or demanding the best of Tokyo and Rome. Just an hour before, to try to forget his loss, Dan had anesthetized himself with an on- bone Veal Parmigiana at the Sinatra Restaurant at the Wynn, washed down by a couple of Hendrick's martinis and was feeling guilty for going so far off training so fast. Perhaps Hicks was right, he didn't have the drive, the discipline. He couldn't imagine Novak Djokovic being so wanton, even after he had lost to Sam Querrey at Wimbledon, that monumental fall after winning four grand slams in a row, unprecedented since the days of Laver. What was he doing? He had sacrificed his life for nothing.

He decided to head back to his room and get a good night's sleep - there was nothing more to do - when a familiar figure jumped off the gondola that was just pulling up in front of him. It was Gombo. He walked straight up to Gelber.

"Is good ride, Mr. Dan. Want to take?" He gestured back to the gondola. "My treat."

Dan ignored him and asked the obligatory question. "What the hell are you doing here?"

"Saw match. I gave you wrong pill."

"Which one? You gave me several."

"Namche Bazaar. Come. Come with me."

He led a flummoxed Dan into a nearby cigar shop of the type frequented by those high-rollers, Chinese and otherwise. Gombo immediately ordered a Churchill. "Not for you," he grinned at Dan, while clipping the end. "You in training." He took a puff and gestured Dan on into a private smoking room. "Not long. Bad for lungs," Gombo remonstrated while exhaling a seemingly endless plume of smoke as if he had actually inhaled the over-sized stogie. "Sit. Sit." Still not sure whether he was glad or horrified to see the Nepali, Dan sank into a leather armchair. "You play good but lose," said Gombo. "My fault."

"Your fault? I wish it were."

"No, no. You have strokes. Most excellent one-hand backhand - like Federer."

"Federer? What do you know about tennis?"

"I big fan of tennis. Many years. Like movie Bobby Riggs and Jean King too. Too bad audience not go."

"They're not going to anything anymore."

"Not your problem. You not want to be writer again. You want to be tennis star." He added that brightly. "Good choice. Better for heart. Next step - Cali!"

"I'm not going."

Gombo stared at him, incredulous. "Cigar smoke make you crazy? I stop and we take gondola ride... Better than original Italy. Good for stomach. No rocking... We talk, then you go Cali. Fly direct from Miami on—"

"Don't bother. I'm not going. Hicks, my coach, says it's over my head at this point. And I promised I'd go to his anniversary."

"Ah, Hicks. Old player in crash. Sad story. Almost die. Anyway, you win Cali. I promise."

"How do you know that?"

Gombo started to laugh. "Why you here? What happen to you in first place? ... So, you lose. You want stop now? Go be old man with bad back and broken pecker? Everything for nothing? ... I tell you - all my fault. I give bad pill. Have better one. Like strong kind from Siberia. Very rare. Hidden in woods with many wolves around. Take one. You win at Cali. After that, sky limit." He reached into his pocket and took out a small glass bottle, passing it over to Dan. The pills inside looked like those he'd seen, though slightly larger. "Take with big glass water... Otherwise, not so good."

Dan was surprised at the size of the stadium at the Tennis Club Cali when, several days later, he first walked into the facility. He shouldn't have been. The tournament, known as the Milo Open, was a serious event in South America. Recent winners had been Joao Souza, the Portuguese number one, and Federico Delbonis, a Davis Cup player, as Hicks had noted, and currently ranked four in Argentina, three slots below the legendary Juan Martin del Potro, winner of the 2009 US Open against the very Roger Federer. Del Potro himself, thankfully, wasn't playing, but others were, including Delbonis, Argentina's Horacio Zeballos, Gerald Melzer from Austria and the Dominican Republic's Victor Estrella Burgos. All these players ranked inside the top 150 - the diminutive Zeballos currently at 67, eking ahead of Delbonis - and from any perspective were superior to the unranked "J. Reynolds" at the bottom of the qualifying draw.

But this did not deter Dan Gelber who, for reasons unclear to him at this point, perhaps it was the new more powerful pills from Siberia or wherever, bounded into the clubhouse with an optimism he had never felt before and, without even a tinge of jet lag from the hours he had spent in the air flying from Vegas to Miami to Cali, even though he awakened at seven a.m. local time with barely three hours sleep. He was on the practice courts by eight, hitting with some local pros, measuring his returns as the ball bounded high from topspin off the red clay. Thank God, Gombo had made him six-two and change. The old Dan would have seen the balls whizzing over his head.

The players were rotating the use of the practice courts and after a couple of hours Dan found himself opposite Dmitry Kuzma, the same Belarusian teenager who had cleaned his clock in Vegas. But this time Dan was more than holding his own, driving the seventeen-year old phenom into corners and leaving him gasping for air. It was as if Dan was not the same player and Kuzma kept looking across at him bewildered. Of course, this was only practice and might not translate to the actual tournament when many, especially Dan in the past, tighten up. But it did. Dan whipped through the qualifying rounds, never losing more than three games in a set and, before he knew it, found himself in the quarter finals of the tournament facing Geraldo Soto, the number one player in Chile ranked 112 in the world. Soto, a veteran at thirty-two, had in his past knocked off two world top ten players, including the renowned David Ferrer at the 2008 Monte Carlo Open. Dan could hardly believe where he was himself and, counting such a deep run in a Challenger tournament already an amazing result, gave himself next to no chance to make it to the semis. But again, he did, measuring his shots and never over-hitting and defeating Soto in a second set tie-breaker 7-2.

That was the night of the Hicks's anniversary and Dan, guilty of course for having run off, forced himself to pick up his cellphone to tender his congratulations and impart the good news of his victory, perhaps as amelioration. His string of good luck continued - was this again due to the pills, did they include pre-destination as well on top of physical prowess - when a certain young woman answered.

"Hello."

"Hello, this is Jay Reynolds. I'm calling from Colombia to —."

"Oh, hi, Jay. This is Molly. How's it going down there? Run into any drug cartels? Though I understand they've sort of cleaned things up."

"Just the FARC."

"Oh, the rebels. I thought they were gone too."

"They are. Actually, it's quite beautiful down here. You ought to come down for the semis."

"The what?"

"The semis. I made the semis."

"How great! Hold on a sec and I'll get dad. He'll be thrilled."

"No, wait, I... was enjoying talking to you. So, I, uh, I guess I'll be back Tuesday - unless I make the finals, which is kind of impossible, considering the opposition."

"Don't say that."

"Okay. False modesty. I'll be back Thursday... I was wondering if you'd like to go out Friday night. You know... I'll take you... I'd like to take you... to dinner."

He was trying to sound more like a shy kid just making it big and less like a divorced man with more experiences than he could remember. It came out somewhere in between. But it didn't matter, she said yes. On top of that, to everyone's amazement, especially the largely Colombian crowd, he won the tournament. It was his first Challengers, raising his ranking to 174 in the world. Dan laughed to himself, as he sat on the plane to Miami, clutching the trophy. That'd show the high school tennis coach Rodney-whatever-his-name-was who kicked him down to the jayvee, doubles no less. It would also show his father who was always critical of his backhand form, even the day he first beat his old man at the age of twelve with a blistering one-hander crosscourt.

Dan didn't like thinking about the latter all that much. Defeating your father was not the kind of triumph you unambiguously enjoyed. You didn't have to be Sophocles to know that. It was fraught with conflicting emotions too obvious to appear in a freshman psychology text let alone some weighty tome from the object relations school of psychoanalysis of the type Dan devoured in midlife to try to find a way out of his problems. But he wasn't in midlife. He was at the beginning again, or close. Deliberately, he shifted his focus to Molly as he changed planes in Miami for Seattle. The most exciting thing in life to him had always been to woo a woman. He was getting another chance after all these years. What should he wear? What restaurant should he take her to? He had his longtime favorite The Brooklyn, but it seemed so old timey, like a men's club, not at all the kind of place an up-and-coming young tennis star would choose.

He couldn't think of a good one, however, and in the end, selected a place even more classical, Canlis, the earliest home of the so-called North-west cuisine, high above Lake Union with the lights of the city sprawling below. It may have become stodgy, but it was still romantic.

"What do you think?" he asked Molly after the waiter had taken their cocktail order.

"Like you said - a bit like the dining room in assisted living." She had a twinkle in her eye as she spoke in a near whisper, so the other patrons couldn't overhear. "But the view is amazing."

"So's the food. I've eaten here twice." But not for forty years he could have added. "How's your father? Is he angry with me for not coming to the anniversary?"

"At first a little... Then he was so astonished you won Cali, he had a coughing fit. I was worried. In his condition, almost anything can set him off and put him right back in the hospital. But he was okay. As excited as kid actually. Though he says to tell you that means you're going to work three times as hard starting Monday."

"Natch."

"He also said to remind you I'm too old for you," she added, breaking into an amused smile that, to Dan, would have melted half of Antarctica.

"It's only a four-year difference." Give or take fifty, Dan thought.

"I'm used to going out with doctors in their thirties and forties. They're about the only people I meet."

"Well, try something different."

"I've been dating one for almost a year now."

Dan felt a sudden contraction in his stomach. "Oh, I… Is it serious?"

"He's a terrific guy. Brazilian. He works with the Walk Again Project in Sao Paulo. They think they've found a way to help people with spinal cord injuries move their legs again, using their thoughts to control the exoskeleton."

"For your dad?"

"Possibly… Everyone in our family's been obsessed with it since the crash. My mother doesn't think it was an accident."

"It was deliberate?" Startled, that was all he could say. "What about you?"

"No, not me… It was… so random, an act of God. But my mother's never been able to handle it. She needs to blame someone… But Dad didn't have an enemy in the world. Still doesn't. It was hard to process for all of us. My father was headed for the top ten. Who knows how good he could have been?"

"An all-time great, maybe…" Dan Gelber wondered if Gombo might be able to help her father but had no idea how to arrange that. In any case, it would ruin everything at this point.

The waiter arrived with the drinks. "Cheers," Molly said, lifting hers.

"Cheers."

They clicked glasses. She took an usually long swallow and put hers down. "To answer your question about Antonio, it's serious on his end. He wants to marry me. I love who he is and what he does, but… I don't love him."

"So, marry me."

Molly started laughing. "What're you saying?"

"You heard me." Dan grinned.

"You're not serious."

"It'd be a Casablanca situation. Only this time Rick gets the girl, not Victor Laszlo."

"I never saw Casablanca. I know - it's embarrassing. Our generation." Her eyes widened. "You saw it?"

"Lots of times… well actually just twice," he hastened to add. "On the late show." Did they still have that? "I mean on Netflix…. Bogart gives up the love of his life for a guy who's going to save France from the Nazis." He looked straight at her. "I know it sounds crazy, but I really am serious."

"Oh, come on, Jay. We hardly know each other… Besides, you have to concentrate on your tennis."

"The tennis will take care of itself… Molly, I'm not sure I entirely know why… it's almost magical… and I know it's sounds really arrogant, but I wouldn't be surprised if I win a few Masters 1000 tournaments next year like Indian Wells or Rome. Maybe even Wimbledon and the US Open."

"Really?"

"I don't blame you for being skeptical. You should be. But it doesn't matter. It will be more of a surprise when it happens. And I'd love to have you by my side when I do it."

She hesitated moment, almost frowning. "Why?"

"Why? … Maybe it's because you're gorgeous, brilliant…caring, obviously… a dream come true. I knew it the moment I saw you… I'd love for you to be the mother of my children." The last he blurted out. Well, he had blurted out everything, but that last more so — before it occurred to him that he might not be able to procreate the second time around. And without children, he knew well from bitter experience, most marriages were glorified shack-ups. Both parties could walk out the door at any moment.

"You're funny," she said. "You'd never think you were twenty-two."

"I guess I'm what they call 'an old soul.'"

"I like that," she said.

"Anyway, I empathize with what happened to your family. My parents died in a fire when I was a little boy." Why was he lying to this woman? But he had no choice. He already told the same thing to her father when he had asked the normal questions about Dan's background.

"I feel for you. That must've been terrible."

"Yeah… it was… Look, I'm sorry. Forget what I said."

"About what?"

"The marriage thing. I was … too impetuous. It's always been one of my faults."

"Always?" She broke into an amused smile. "An 'old soul' shouldn't do that."

"I think we should order."

"Yes."

They sat there a moment before picking up the menu.

That night Dan was unsure what to do when he dropped Molly off. Should he make a pass? He decided not to. It wasn't just that he was confused by current mores or even that he feared rejection. He preferred not to. The courtship experience, whatever era it was from, however outdated it might be, was too pleasurable to rush. One night stands were for college kids. He might have been that age but he wasn't really that age. And he wanted to avoid the mistakes of the past. This was to be his second chance after all. But what did that mean, he wondered, as he stared at the ceiling in bed, unable to sleep? Could a relationship actually last? When he married his first wife he thought it was forever, but it was in the middle of the free love era and doomed, although neither of them knew it at the time, from the start. Few couples really could have withstood or did withstand the pressure of those days, especially living in Los Angeles with the Doors playing at the Whiskey and the streets lined with twentieth century foxes. It was too irresistible, at least Dan told himself that. If he hadn't indulged he would have been completely out of it, a failed member of his generation. Be there or be square, as the saying went. So on with self-indulgence masquerading as sophistication. Not that he was alone. His ex was doing the same thing, subject as she was to the same forces. No good came of it. It was only a question of who would serve the papers first. Buffeted by the fallout, Dan bounced into a second marriage just weeks after his divorce became official, realizing it was a mistake but unable to get himself to do anything about it as he stood at the makeshift altar on a Malibu beach, staring out at the Pacific with sitar music playing. His agent was his best man. A dozen hours or so later he was honeymooning in a tropical hut suspended over the water in Bora-Bora, jet lagged and unable to sleep, compulsively reading *The Name of The Rose* in the bathroom, determined at all cost to discover the novel's MacGuffin - ironically the permanent destruction of Aristotle's Comedy - instead of fornicating or even spooning with his second wife. It too was over before it started.

Not surprisingly, in his second life and what would putatively be his third marriage, he wondered if could he make one last? Was he even capable of monogamy? He wanted to think so, but there was no indication he could be. He had no evidence to offer himself. He had wandered too often, but so had the women he had been with. For all the talk of men being the compulsive adulterers, preprogrammed by evolution, their philandering always took place with someone else and that someone else was a female fully conscious of what she was doing, assuming, in the modern parlance with which he could barely keep up, you were cisgendered. For Dan, there had been a number of those females. He wasn't exceptional in that way, he thought, particularly for someone who worked in Hollywood or in the arts in general. Of course, he had been a writer, low on the food chain as those things go, but on the chain nevertheless. Could he get off it? Did he want to? Sports stars were not exactly immune. Gombo had not given him guidelines and Dan had not even thought to pose the question at the time. And that assumed Gombo would have known the answer. He was just what they called in Hollywood a hyphenate: Ayurvedic doctor hyphen shaman. Or perhaps it all came down to the fact that marriage was an institution originated when life expectancy was twenty-five.

Still something in Dan automatically programmed him toward it. It was in his DNA. Some women just made him want to make babies. He felt that with Molly, although he readily admitted to himself that he hardly knew her. He was falling in love with an image, just as he had in his previous life and this time it was all too clear to him. But it didn't stop him. That was the way of the world. It was where Eros lived. For those magic moments it was the most important thing in life.

But tennis was important too—and growing. Having won two Challenger tournaments in a row, he was ready for the real ATP tournaments now and played in his first one at Del Rey Beach, reaching the semi-finals and surprising everyone. Even Hicks was impressed.

"You could have won," he said. "You were right there. That last backhand hit the tape and trickled the wrong way." Dan wondered about that himself. He had hit the backhand with considerable top and was sure it would go over. But it bounced up high off the tape and skittered back to his side, giving his opponent the game and the match in three sets. "Still, you're doing incredible… for a lazy bum," Derek continued. "You barely practice. Do you know Andy Murray used to run fifteen miles a day - in the sand? So don't get cocky. Del Rey was just a 250. The prize money's hardly worth the plane tickets. Wait'll you get to the 500s and the 1000s and the competition stiffens up, not to mention the majors. You're gonna have to start assembling a team - a trainer and a physio, at least. Probably a business manager. Maybe an assistant coach. I'll find them for you. But the good ones aren't going to fly economy. And when you're playing the French Open, they want to be at the Ritz."

"I'll cover it."

"And stop calling my daughter every night. I know it's lonely on the road, but some people can hear through the wall."

He was right. It was lonely. He was playing the Copa Claro when he really started to notice it. The tournament was down in Buenos Aires and normally that would have been exciting, but he had no one to share the experience with. The other players seemed like kids - they really were to Dan - and Hicks didn't want to go out at night. Tango joints weren't much fun for people in wheel chairs and the older man, who was actually the younger man, got tired from the day's exertion coaching "Jay Reynolds". This was true although Dan won that tournament and went on to win the next one as well in Rio. That was a 500 event, Dan's first, his victory accompanied by a ton of ranking points and a payday just shy of sixty thousand for two weeks work. He was on his way.

By now Hicks, true to his word, had assembled a team for him. The trainer was an Austrian body builder named Horst who had worked with Arnold Schwarzenegger when they were young but missed out on the movie (or the political) career. The physio was Prem, a retired Thai kick boxer turned sports dietitian who gave the most incredible shiatsu massages Dan had ever experienced. He put Dan on a stretching regime fit for a dancer at the Kirov while preparing him gluten free meals laced with enough creatine monohydrate to bench press the Empire State building. For a business manager Hicks brought in Isaac Glasser, a former CAA sports agent out on his own now as an independent contractor. Dan thought he recognized him from the agency corridors years ago, but of course didn't' say anything. He was mostly out scouting big endorsement contracts anyway. Dan thought that was premature, not that he cared that much, but he was too astonished at the last member of the team Hicks added to dwell on it. Andy Roddick had agreed to be his assistant coach on a part-time basis, the way Agassi had signed on with Djokovic.

"That's amazing," said Dan. "Why on Earth would he want to do that?"

"Andy wants an American to finally break through. He doesn't trust Jack Sock. Talented with a great forehand, but too erratic. Besides, you're younger."

"Only by a couple years." Dan was finally becoming able to refer to his supposed age without thinking of his real one. It was sort of like learning to think in French.

"Andy'll be invaluable by your side in the majors. He's been there in a big way. Maybe he wants to make up for that famous Wimbledon final when he came within a whisker of beating Federer. You were about twelve I would guess."

Dan nodded. Who could forget that heartbreak when Roddick went down 16-14 in the fifth set, still the longest Wimbledon final in games played? "That was about the end of his career, wasn't it? At least emotionally. Who could bounce back from that?"

"The truly great…. Anyway, don't worry about it. He won't be with us for a month or so. Meanwhile, you've got your biggest hill to climb."

True enough. Looming ahead was Dan's first Masters 1000 - the BNP Paribas Open in Indian Wells, California, the most prestigious American tennis tournament other than the US Open. He was ranked number 32 in the world and would be seeded 29.

VII

THE TESTING

Dan slept with Molly for the first time two nights before Indian Wells. They were staying at La Quinta, a posh desert resort in the Spanish style about twenty minutes' drive from the tournament site. In his previous life he had lived through the uncomfortable truth that you rarely had the hottest sex with the people you loved, but this was more than good enough, so good in fact that they had awakened early - about six a. m. - for a third round, feeling about as enraptured as he could remember, about to declare eternal love, when they were interrupted by a knock on their bungalow door.

"Who is it?" said Dan, sitting up in bed. Startled, Molly reached for her robe.

"WADA, Mr. Reynolds. Open up, please."

WADA... WADA.... Dan searched in his memory for the acronym. Oh, yes - the World Anti-Doping Agency. "Just a second," he cried out, suddenly panicking but realizing he should do his best not to show it. It was one of those spot tests for athletes he'd heard about. Doping was a serious matter, he knew. Russia had been banned from the Olympics for it. In tennis, some had suspected Nadal for a long time because of his muscular appearance and incredible endurance. But what could they get Dan for? It was obvious. The first thing Dan Gelber thought of—indeed he did so immediately - was Gombo and his stash of Himalayan herbs. But how would they have known about that? Maybe it was something else, he tried to convince himself, something more conventional. Was there anything to fear? He had had half a margarita the previous night but that was about it. He hadn't snorted cocaine in about fifteen years, maybe more. Marijuana bored him. LSD was back in college, literally in another century. And steroids, when he took them only once in his previous life as an experiment, gave him heart palpitations. So, all that was left was indeed the herbs. But how could they possibly know what they were, Dan Gelber repeated to himself. He didn't know what they were, even if they were still in his body, which seemed unlikely. WADA was after those same steroids or human growth hormone, he had read, or that blood-pumping stuff used by the Russian army they had caught Sharapova with. What was it? He remembered - meldonium. Dan Gelber pulled on his pajama bottoms while doing a good job, he told himself, of staying calm, went to the door and opened it. "Good morning."

A man and a woman, both dressed incongruously in suits against the desert background, stood at the entryway. The woman had a medical brief-case. "Good morning. May we come in."

"Of course. This is Ms. Hicks." Dan gestured to Molly who was sitting up in bed.

"How do you do?" said the woman. "I am Dr. Withers. This is Mr. Harold Abelson of the ATP. We are sorry to disturb you at this hour, but we must conduct a routine PED check." PED for performance enhancing drugs. The forms he had been given were coming back to him now. He hadn't paid much attention, probably blocked them out.

"Pleased to meet you," said Abelson, extending his hand. "Congratu-lations on your rapid rise."

"Just lucky," Dan said, reflecting on the fact that an actual official of the Association of Tennis Professionals had accompanied the doctor from WADA. Well, maybe that was normal.

"No, no. It's quite remarkable. Almost unprecedented... Out of nowhere," the official added with a smile.

"I'll probably go out in the first round here, so it won't be so amaz-ing anymore."

"Maybe I should leave," said Molly.

"It's not necessary Ms. Hicks," Dr. Withers replied, opening her brief-case. "All we need is Mr. Reynolds to step into the bathroom for a moment." She handed Dan a small graduated cup for a urine sample. "Be sure to fill up to the line, seal and sign your name on the label. We'll do the rest. We won't need a blood test at this time."

Dan Gelber tried not to fixate on the words "at this time" while walking into the bathroom, shutting the door behind him and unbuttoning his fly. The stream of piss came out with the consistent, pain free, flow of a man in his early twenties. Dan was well used to this ease by now, but he still couldn't help marveling at the change. Sometimes, he would stand at the edge of a cliff and piss over it, making a giant arc, just as he did as a kid, to see how far it would go. In this instance, the fascination almost caused him to overflow the graduated cup. He closed the lid at the last second and stared at the clear yellow fluid, straining to see if there were any impurities, any evidence of the pills Gombo had given him in a small bottle of ochre-tinted glass. That bottle, currently half filled, was buried in a compartment at the back of his suitcase, just beneath a dirty clothes bag. But there were no telltale impurities in evidence in the cup as he held it up to the light, not that he would have recognized them if there were. It amused him for a moment that he could be playing a trick on WADA, coming in under the radar with a secret elixir from Namche Bazaar - something new for the world of professional sports. He would take big time tennis by storm using a mysterious potion leftover from the hunter-gatherer era.

Indeed, it was big time, that tennis, he noticed a couple of hours later on the practice court. More people were watching him warm up than were ever in the stands for his previous matches. For all his previous successes in exotic locales, those were minor tournaments in the global sense, barely reported outside their countries except on obscure tennis websites. This was the first time he was getting an inkling of what it felt to be a genuine sports star. He liked it, although it still had the sensation of an out of body experience, not the real him, undeserved. The real him was still the first him he wanted to forget, the him that could barely make the high school team.

Even so, and ironically considering what had happened, back then, as a child, Dan Gelber had not taken sports that seriously, and not just because he wasn't particularly good at them, but because he didn't think it a sufficiently intellectual pursuit, not worthy. Though, like other boys, he idolized sports stars, he also slightly disdained them as dumb jocks. Mickey Mantle, Dan's hero at age six, was, despite the center fielder's extraordinary gifts, the ability practically to hit a ball clean out of Yankee Stadium ambi-dextrously (he had seen it), clearly a redneck doofus out of Nowheresville,

Oklahoma who had personality issues and drank too much. But tennis players were different, even back in Dan's childhood. Laver and Rosewall were distinguished gentlemen of international renown, both as amateurs and, later, pioneering professionals. Pancho Gonzalez looked and acted like a movie star, Riccardo Montalbán or Desi Arnaz, and had a romantic story, emerging, as he did, from the streets of East LA. And that was before the era of modern communications. Now the top players had turned into global ambassadors of sport and virtually everything else from philanthropy to international relations. How many languages did Roger Federer speak? He was seemingly the world's most elegant man, creating schools for indigent South African children while being chosen chief spokesman for Rolex watches, the luxury brand of luxury brands. Federer emanated more class, it was assumed, than even the royal family. Dan had seen him in the corridor leading to the locker room and briefly nodded to him. The maestro nodded in return, and Dan wondered for a moment what his gang back at the Hancock Tennis Club would think if they could see him now. The BNP Paribas venue was only slightly more than two hours' drive into the desert from Los Angeles and several of the members went every year, Dan among them. But their chances of recognizing him as a player, he reasoned, were almost non-existent. Still, anything was possible, the child being the father of the man and all that, even if the child were half a foot taller than the man with different colors of hair and eyes.

Dan didn't have to wait long to find out. He was playing his second round match on one of the outer courts - not on Stadium 1 with its 16,000 seats, that would come later - that are more intimate and often thought by fans to make for some of the finest viewing in the sport, when he heard a short burst sound from a camera's motor drive just as he was about to serve. His concentration broken, he paused and looked over his shoulder to see his old doubles partner from the tennis club Ben in the third row, photographing him through the telephoto lens of a DSLR. Ben seemed momentarily embarrassed by his faux pas and sheepishly put the camera down. Dan smiled, remembering Ben was an inveterate shutterbug and seemingly photographed half the players in the tournament on one trip they had made together a few years before. Dan nodded to him pleasantly, then resumed serving, hitting a clean ace down the T. In a short while, he had won the match against the number two player from Taiwan in straight sets. He was in the third round of what was the fifth largest tennis tournament in the world. It happened so fast - it was almost too easy. But then it was supposed to be, if one were to believe Gombo and his powers.

That evening, a spectacular magenta sunset played out against the mountains surrounding the Coachella Valley. Walking with Molly across the palm-lined grounds known as the Indian Wells Tennis Garden, Dan Gelber felt almost god-like. He could feel the buzz of the crowd, the excitement as they waited for the night matches. Fans pointed at him and waved. "Great job, Jay. You da man - America's hope!" one yelled. "Show Tsonga what for," said another, referring to Gelber's third round opponent, the number fifteen player in the world from France. A little girl ran over with her father, extending one of those giant foam tennis balls for him to sign. It was already the twelfth - or was it the twentieth - time he had been asked for his autograph that day. The signatures and the attendant selfies were getting to be automatic. "Jay Reynolds," he scrawled with a smiley face that he added for kids. He didn't once forget and sign Dan Gelber.

Just as he finished drawing that smiley face and was returning the felt pen to the girl, Ben walked up to him with an abashed expression. "Mr. Reynolds... I'm so sorry. I have to apologize for that photo. I just can't help myself. She says I should leave my camera at home." He gestured to his wife Faye who stood alongside him.

"No problem. You may have inspired an ace..."

"Well, something good happened from my mistake then, but somehow I think it was you."

"Not me necessarily."

"Don't be foolish. You played great ... I'm Ben Lipkin and this is my wife Faye."

"How do you do? Jay Reynolds." Dan boldly thrust his hand out to the people he knew very well from umpteen dinners, doubles matches and trips to the movies. It would be a test. "Pleased to meet you."

"Likewise," said Ben. "Been following your meteoric career. Impressive!"

"And a one-handed backhanded too," said Faye. "You don't see a lot of those now with players your age."

"I'm just an old school guy," said Dan.

"He really is," Molly added. "I can promise you."

"This is my, uh, fiancée Molly Hicks."

"I am?"

"If you want to be."

"That's interesting."

"Are we intruding on something here?" said Ben.

"No, but I am." Another man had walked up. It was Dan's new business manager Isaac Glasser. "Hey, buddy!" He clapped Dan on the back. "Mr. Popularity... can I borrow you a minute? I've got a surprise. You were being watched during the last match."

"That's for sure."

"No, no. By someone important. The Nike rep. He wants to make a deal."

"Already? I'm only in the third round."

"They think they're late. I told them we were talking to Adidas." He gestured toward a man standing about fifty feet away. "Hey, Zack, over here!"

It was his son! What a bizarre turn of events, how unbelievably extraordinary, Dan Gelber thought. How was he going to deal with this? "He's the Nike rep?"

"He's new," Glasser lowered his voice as Zack approached. "To our advantage."

"Hey, Jay, great playing. What a future... I'm Zack Gelber." He was pumping Dan's hand who was feeling lightheaded and could barely speak. "Nike's man here at Indian Wells, but I'm sure Isaac told you. You okay?"

"Fine, fine. Nice to meet you."

"We're prepared to have you fleece us if you wear our shorts - just keep winning."

"Zack Gelber, my God! You're Dan's son!" said Ben. "We met a few years ago, remember? At the club Christmas party."

"Yes, of course."

"How are you?" Faye clutched his hand. "What a tragedy what happened to your father."

"So awful," Ben added. "If only I could've done something but he never told me he was going to the Himalayas.... " He shook his head in commiseration, then clutched Zack's shoulder.

"That's okay. He only told me at the last minute. He just went.... Kind of like him really."

Dan suddenly felt like a dead rat had been deposited in the pit of his stomach and left to rot. "He probably had his reasons," he said.

"I guess.... They never even found his body. Just that water-logged backpack. If the passport wasn't in plastic wrap, we would never have known anything," said Zack, staring moodily at the ground for a second before resuming salesman mode. "Anyway, that's yesterday. We're here for tennis, no? And dinner at Nobu's." He put on a happy face, pointing up toward the grandstand location of the famous sushi restaurant. Wrapped in teak down to its reception desk it had become almost as hard a ticket as the matches themselves. "I booked a table, hoping you could make it. For five, of course, to include your friend here who I understand is the daughter of the legendary Derek Hicks, a man I personally thought was going to be one of the greats of the game."

"Wasn't he before your time?" said Dan. How the hell could Zack have known about Hicks if he hadn't? Probably doing his homework for the hard sell. "And I would have figured you for more of soccer fan as a boy than tennis."

"You know," said Zack, looking mildly surprised. "That's actually true. I was a demon soccer player as a kid. Couldn't stay away from it. You would have thought I was Mexican or Italian. Problem was I, um, didn't quite have the foot speed. So here I am pushing designer sneakers. It's not as glamorous but everyone could use a good pair, right?" he added with a grin. "Every kid a Jay Reynolds!"

In a certain way, Dan Gelber realized later that night, he wanted Zack to discover him, to realize he who he was, at least part of him did. He threw out other hints over dinner - Zack joked that Jay was almost as good a psychic as he was a tennis player - though Dan didn't bring up anything about Zack's children. He didn't ask anything that would hint he knew about his grandson Peter and his problems. That would have been too much. Inside, however, Dan Gelber was turning over painful images from his past like pictures on a nearly endless deck of cards, unsure whether to suppress the memories they engendered or let them wash over him until they exhausted themselves in the manner of some form of meditation he vaguely remembered. Vipassana? Little Zack breaking into sobs and then throwing a tantrum, kicking his legs on the floor and screaming he was going to die, when hearing of his parents' impending divorce, his mother later putting Zack on the phone in a well-rehearsed plea for his father to come back even though it was unlikely she really wanted him back - she just wanted Dan to *say* he wanted to come back. And on it went, a nightmare song of the 1980s when an entire generation was out to self-actualize at the expense of their children, narcissism run amuck under the flag of free love rationalized by some worn out or restructured ideas from Karl Marx. Still, Zack had made it through all right, more than all right, it seemed to Dan Gelber after all. He had misjudged things in his previous life. Here he was in reality a competent young marketing exec for Nike with a family of his own, whatever difficulties they might be having. All families had difficulties and there were many worse. That was what Dan Gelber told himself. Nature would right itself.

Nevertheless, Gelber thought he had to avoid, in fact knew he had to avoid, even at all costs, the prospective Nike deal in order not to put himself in this position again, to able to forget his past life as much he could, hopefully eventually to annihilate it. But Isaac was sitting there, and it would have seemed strange indeed overtly to push away an offer from the most famous maker of sports apparel on the planet, not that such an offer was made, explicitly. So, Dan sat there pretending to be interested but not over-reacting while Zack conjured what it would be like to have an All-American line of tennis clothing in his name (Jay Reynolds warm-up jackets with his personal logo?). Domestic fans had been lusting for such a memento since the glory days of Sampras and Agassi. A series of signature rackets, not just one, could be in the offing. Nike could make a deal with Wilson or Head. Coming from his son, this was making Dan Gelber increasingly uncomfortable, approaching the point of nausea. He had eaten Nobu's sushi several times before in his previous life, gobbling it down to the last possible rice grain and ginger slice, only to leave wanting to start all over again, but tonight he had no appetite. He excused himself to go to the bathroom three times during dinner, not to vomit but to collect himself.

"Are you okay? You seem depressed," said Molly as they lay in bed.

"I'm fine."

"I mean you're in the third round of Indian Wells and you look as if you've seen a ghost."

"They're always there, aren't they?" Dan forced a little laugh. "Maybe it's my background. I've been looking it up."

"On ancestry dot com?"

"Haven't done it."

"We should send in our DNA. Lots of couples do. What do you think yours would say?"

"Ninety-six percent Ashkenazi Jew."

Molly started to laugh. "More like ninety-six percent Swedish lumberjack."

, "Hey, don't stereotype. There are tall Jews. Sandy Koufax."

"Who?"

"Never mind… Just someone I read about in a sports book when I was a kid. I memorized the stats of all the players. …horribly cisgendered of me."

"No need to apologize. I'm cisgendered too…. A few years in medical school forces you to go back to it."

"I can imagine." They lay there a moment. He turned over in bed and faced her, telling himself what a schmuck he was to dwell in the past and not focus on the here and now. Look at what was in front of him. "I love you," he said. "You're the most amazing woman I have ever been with."

"How many is that, precocious one?" She tapped him playfully on the nose.

"Okay, not that many. But you're still amazing. I can't believe I'm with you." He kissed her on the lips. As he would have written in a script in his past life, it deepened.

But after they made love, he lay awake for the rest of the night.

Not that it impeded his play on the court the next day. Dan played "like a man possessed." And quite possibly he was. The match with Tsonga lasted less than an hour and was on Stadium Two that was filled to capacity with eight thousand fans, among them Oracle founder Larry Ellison who bought the tournament for a hundred million and poured hundreds more into the facilities over the years. The entrepreneur sat, as he almost always did, in the front row next to some gorgeous female barely half his age. Just three rows behind him was Gombo.

Concentrating on the game, Dan hadn't noticed the Nepali until he was serving for the match well-ahead 5-1 in the final set, causing Dan to double fault, though he won the game on the next point with a solid volley that skidded unanswerably off the line. Gombo was there again for the quarter-finals when Dan defeated Roberto Bautista-Agut in a closer match, though, truth to tell, he never felt in danger, even when the Spaniard broke Dan's serve and took the lead in the second set. Hicks, sitting with Molly in Dan's team's box, seemed worried, drumming his fingers on the wheels of his chair, but Dan looked from him to Gombo, who sat there calmly, and was reassured. Methodically, Dan played crosscourt to Batista-Agut's backhand, sometimes twenty shots in a row, biding his time textbook style until one of his opponent's returns fell just a tiny bit short and he could redirect the ball down the line for a winner. In fifty-eight minutes, that match too was booked. Dan was in the semi-finals of the most prestigious Masters tournament in tennis, second only in importance - and ranking points - to the Grand Slams themselves.

That semi-final match was on Stadium One filled that day to its capacity of sixteen thousand one hundred that made it the third biggest arena in the sport after the Arthur Ashe in New York and the O2 in London. Dan's opponent was Sasha Zverev, the young German said by many to be the natural heir to the aging "Big Four" - Federer, Nadal, Djokovic and Murray. At six foot six without any discernible weaknesses and a killer serve, he was a formidable opponent. And he proved so, racing through the beginning of the first set 4-0. Dan tried hard. He felt good, played aggressively as he knew he had to against a player of this quality, but he just couldn't get untracked. He glanced up at his box where his team, particularly Molly, endeavored to be supportive with encouraging signs and fist pumps, even as Dan's passing shots were consistently falling just outside the lines, his crosscourt shots always ending up somehow in the alley or barely dipping into the tape, hanging in suspended animation on top only to bounce back on his side. When he looked up toward Gombo, seated once again in the third row, the Ayurvedic doctor appeared disinterested, occasionally looking down at a book in his lap.

Dan took the time while changing sides to reflect on his situation and alter his game plan. This was the advice given by Hicks, but he had known it himself for years. He might not have been a great player in his previous life, but he understood enough of the strategy. Maybe he could tempt an unsuspecting Zverev into defeating himself. Grind it out Brad Gilbert style - win ugly. Dan came out playing more conservatively and not attempting to paint the lines, as he had, but the ball still traveled barely out. Several times it almost seemed guided, as if at the last moment a gust had come up out of nowhere to carry the ball just beyond or outside the line, but there was no wind in the desert that day. It was hot and dry and unworldly still. The calls were so close that twice Dan used the Hawk-Eye system to challenge, but each time the GPS showed the ball out by the slightest of margins, millimeters. The separation between ball and line on the video screen was almost invisible, but it was there.

Each time, the crowd gasped, temporarily siding with Dan who was having such horrible luck. He was, after all, the home boy, battling a more highly ranked European almost exactly the same age. What could be the explanation for this never-ending run of near misses? Was this some mysterious *force majeure* or something extra-terrestrial? Some fans shared looks of bafflement - how could it be happening? Even Zverev seemed surprised as a passing shot way out of his reach and on which he had given up flew out at the last second. Surely this couldn't occur again. The odds were spectacular. But on the next exchange it did. What looked like a sure winning serve of Dan's, a certain ace, was called out by the linesman. It almost seemed as if the tennis ball had turned into a whiffle ball at the last second, danced around, and landed just beyond the line. Or was it on the line? Whatever the case, Dan was out of challenges for the set with no choice but to prepare to hit his second serve with the score five-love, forty-fifteen against him. He looked up at Gombo who was standing now, his book closed, making his way to the exit to the annoyance of the spectators in the neighboring rows. Dan watched him for a moment, then tossed the ball up, observed the seams carefully as one is supposed to do as it turned in the air, slowing time, before deliberately lowering his head and serving the ball into the net, delivering the set, uncontested, to Zverev. The audience gasped in astonishment as Dan ran off the court, yelling to the umpire that he was taking a legal bathroom break.

He caught up with Gombo in the lower corridor, grabbing the Nepali by the arm and yanking him through a doorway marked "staff only" into in area filled with maintenance equipment.

"Okay, what's going on? Why're you sabotaging me?"

"You cannot make look easy, Mr. Dan. Maybe they take blood sample next time, not just urine. Then you lose all."

"They'd recognize your herb?"

"Who knows?"

"You should. You can bend balls like Uri Geller bends spoons."

"Old trick. Not always work."

"Anyway, I don't want to win if it's only you. What does it mean then?"

"Everyone have gift. Nobody win by self." He held up the book he had been reading. "Is written in Upanishad: "As your will is, so is your deed. As your deed is, so is your destiny."

"And my destiny is what? To rise like a shooting star and be tortured by you? Why didn't you tell me I would remember everything from my past?"

"You did not ask."

"It's making me miserable."

"If that is problem, then forget it."

"How do you do that?"

'You have fun. Nothing to do about past. Already happened… But don't win the finals. Go too quick."

"How could I win? I'd be playing Rafael Nadal."

"Don't worry. You could. Lose now. Win at French…. As John McEnroe say – 'Be relentless point-for-point.'"

"Where'd you hear that?"

"Tennis Channel very popular in Reseda."

VIII
FAME

PAGE SIX

TENNIS WUNDERKIND HITS PARIS WITH NEW LOVE

Not since Jackie O or even the Normandy invasion has Paris been so abuzz with the arrival of an American the way it is about US tennis hope Jay Reynolds and his brainy, gorgeous paramour Dr. Molly Hicks…

D an had been on the NY Post's Page Six a few times before as Jay Reynolds. He had even once been on it as Dan Gelber, although way at the bottom, when he dated an actress for six weeks, feeling awkward the whole time before she dumped him (he was relieved). But never on top like this. Now he liked it, in a disembodied sort of way. Was this really him? Nevertheless, the words of Gombo had taken effect. The purpose of life was to have fun. Enjoy yourself for tomorrow you die - for the second time. He assumed that would be his quotient. As the victories on the tennis court mounted up, with the attendant adulation, the cares of his first life faded in the distance. He could build a second life of perfection.

And as Gombo had predicted, Paris had shown the way. Dan rode with Molly into the City of Light from de Gaulle in a Mercedes-Maybach

Pullman 600, an update of the classic limo, as he played with its equipment, the partition window separating the passengers from the driver that turned opaque at the press of a button, or fiddled with its Dolby version 4 surround sound music system that responded to voice commands in a dozen languages. He considered calling up Piaf or Aznavour but realized Molly probably would not have heard of them and it would only provoke an uncomfortable line of questions that could unmask his more than nominal familiarity with the city. "Your pick," he said. A child of her generation, Molly chose Alicia Keys and Usher singing "My Boo". Dan liked it.

He was more or less oblivious to the passing nightmare of the Paris suburbs, a sight that so disturbed him in his previous life, the endless squalid government housing with its Arabic graffiti interrupted by the recognizable roman letters NTMJ, *nique ta mère juif*, fuck your mother Jew, that signaled the decline of a once grand civilization.

Or was it ever that great. Dan Gelber wondered? He first came to Paris when he was quite young—eleven years old—with his parents. His mother was a Francophile and had attended some of her high school years there. That was not long before the Nazi invasion and the Vichy government and, as he grew older, Gelber would ask her about what that was like. Was she in danger? She would recount stories that gave the impression she was under constant peril, but gradually Dan suspected, indeed was pretty certain, they were exaggerated.

Nevertheless, he grew up with a romantic attraction for France and the glory days of *La Résistance*, even if he thought there was something phony and self-serving about it all. He went back numerous times, well over a dozen, learned the language well enough to speak it without an excessive American accent and had a couple of French girlfriends between wives. One of them, a movie producer he met at Cannes, lasted for a while. But she was married and Gelber eventually discovered he was not French enough to successfully negotiate the seemingly ubiquitous local habit of a double life. So he ended it.

None of this, of course, did he relate to Molly as they motored into the city. Soon enough the familiar arcades of the Rue Royal loomed in front of him.

"Wow, gorgeous, isn't it? Just like the post cards," he smiled broadly at Molly, who actually was seeing Paris for the first time. "Or the movies."

"It didn't look so terrific near the airport."

"Like a lot of cities these days…Hey, don't be so dreary. This is supposed to be the most romantic city on the planet - or so I'm told. And we're together… Look, the Louvre… that is the Louvre, isn't it?"

"It must be. It's got that modern pyramid everyone talks about. I. M. Pei," said Molly.

"Who?" He said innocently.

"The architect. Chinese-American. He won the Pritzker and a lot of other things."

"Oh…. interesting."

"So you don't know everything after all!" She laughed and poked him playfully, looking more than slightly pleased, maybe relieved. Gelber did not disabuse of her of the notion. He didn't like lying to this woman. Not in the slightest. But he didn't seem to have a choice. "Okay, I'm ready to be romantic," she continued, kissing him on the lips. "Just a little jetlagged."

"Not to worry. This is Paris. I bet you can get a fabulous cappuccino at our hotel." He knew damn well she could. They were booked into the Intercontinental Le Grand opposite the opera house. He had never stayed there on his many trips to the city, but he had had more than one cappuccino at the hotel's restaurant, the legendary Café de la Paix. For the better part of a year he would go there every morning to work on a screenplay that was never made. It didn't matter. It was part of the zeitgeist. In a short while, they were pulling up at the hotel.

"What the fuck're you doing, hitting with a stiff wrist. This isn't the 1970s!" The next morning Dan looked over at Hicks who was seated in his wheelchair between Molly and his physio on the edge of the practice court. "That's the way they played before you were born. You in dreamland?"

"More or less."

"Well, get over it…. Something wrong with your arm? We'll get you a mess—"

"No, no. It's okay?"

"Then loosen the wrist. Put top on the ball. This is Roland Garros, if you haven't noticed. You're on the historic red clay, the *terre battue*. Get some bounce yourself or you're gonna need a pogo stick against Nadal."

"Right, right."

"This is a Grand Slam, amigo. You need to be serious like you've never been. Real intensity, nothing casual or daydreaming through even ten seconds of practice. Otherwise we should all go home." He turned to his daughter. "Am I being too tough on your boyfriend? He's not going out tonight. Coach's orders. In bed by ten... alone."

Molly waved her father off with a grin just as Dan crossed to his right and hit a wicked forehand down the line, loaded with the top that made the ball grab the red clay and spin almost straight upwards, flying over the head of his six-foot four rally partner who could only flail at the ball.

"Now that's how you play the French Open!" said Hicks, banging on his metal arm of his chair in approval. He turned and gave the thumbs up sign to Molly. It had taken a while, but the coach had become reconciled to Dan's relationship with his daughter. Indeed, at this point, Dan suspected he actually approved. On the other hand, Gelber noticed that Hick's health was deteriorating. At least it appeared so. At times his head would be slumped over, eyes closed. At other times he was short of breath, almost gasping. At those moments, Dan Gelber wondered if there were some way in which he could help the poor man, if not via Gombo, some other manner. But he couldn't think of anything and did nothing.

That night Dan took Molly to La Closerie des Lilas. "Hemingway ate here," he said. "It's in 'A Moveable Feast'." He could have added he had eaten there several times himself - with his parents and both his French girlfriends.

"I haven't read it. No time in medical school. Hear it's great though... But I did see that Woody Allen movie," she added with a twinkle.

"'Midnight in Paris'? The only film of his that's made money in decades. It's amusing in a shallow kind of way. I liked the guy who played Buñuel though."

"Who?"

"Luis Buñuel. Spanish filmmaker. Surrealist. Worked with Dali.... 'Viridiana.' 'The Discreet Charm of the Bourgeoisie'." She was drawing a blank. "It's an amazing film. Made in the early seventies. You should see it... But not at a restaurant. The characters all sit on toilet seats while they're eating dinner." What was he doing? It was almost, Dan Gelber realized, as if he were intending to out himself by parading his knowledge, paltry though it was. Was it guilt because he had come here with previous girlfriends, inconsequential as they may have been? Why did he pick this place when there were a thousand other restaurants? Well, it was Paris to him. Or the way he wanted Paris to be.

"You have all these cultural references, but you didn't have time for college. Sometimes I think you secretly went to Yale or Harvard, but you're not telling anyone."

"Princeton." He said, forcing a smile. "Actually, I took a lot of dopey online courses. You can learn about almost anything on YouTube if you want to. How to fix a flat. How to change you iPhone battery. How—"

"What about theology?"

"That too."

"Have you done it?"

"Not much."

"Do you believe in God?"

"Well, there's a show stopper. We haven't even ordered... Anyway, I haven't had the existence of God in my YouTube queue, if that's what you mean. Above my job description, as they say."

"It's not such a strange question if we're going to be together?"

He hesitated, noting her sudden seriousness. In truth, Dan Gelber rarely thought about the issue. He lived in a world where few did. From Hollywood to publishing, God was an inconvenient subject for the most part. Even Passover Seders were more a time to gossip about absent relatives or argue about politics in the midst of the requisite prayers and songs. It had been that way since he was a boy.

"My dad asked me the same thing," Molly continued. "He was curious about you. He became a believer after his accident. "

"One of those near death experiences, huh..." Dan tried to smile, but a cold chill came over him even though they were sitting on the Closerie's patio on a balmy May evening. What was that about? "I don't really know how to answer. Sometimes I do and sometimes I don't. Most of my life I was an atheist."

"Most of your life?" The smile returned. "You mean you were an atheist at five, when you played with your blocks?"

"Er... more or less.... but once in a while I think maybe I'm more like the Haredim."

"The who?"

"Ultra-orthodox Jews. The ones in black hats and heavy overcoats in summer, sometimes fur hats. I don't speak Hebrew, but their name means something like 'those who fear God.'"

"Interesting..... Why are you so afraid of God? Have you done something wrong?" she continued, more playfully.

"Not so far," he replied, although, he might have added, he was in touch with his own fear of what the shrinks called the repetition compulsion. Did it extend into second lives?

"Well then, don't." Now the smile was broader.

"I'm not planning on it," he said, his mind suddenly shifting back to the Himalayas again. Dan Gelber was watching his red backpack bounding down the mountainside into the rapids and then disappearing with his old identity. Where had it gone? Would it come back to haunt him? Once more he heard the sound of the siren, someone shouting "Go! Go!" Was it Gombo or who? He felt for a second as if he really were one of the Haredim. He was afraid of God, temporarily anyway. "You know what I think we should do?" he said. "Start a foundation."

"A foundation? That's noble."

"Federer and Djokovic have done it. We should do something good with all the money I'm going to make."

"You're going to make that much? You sound so certain. Why don't you—"

"No, no. It is... for certain.... Believe me. I know..."

"Okay. Confidence is a good thing, I guess."

"It's more than that. Trust me... We should give back. We have to. Maybe start a charity to do something for your favorite cause that is now mine too... walking again." Dan reached across the table and took her hand. Off in the distance he could hear the sound of French jazz violin, Jean-Luc Ponty. It was at once nostalgic and hypnotic. "I'd really like to do that. ... It's my duty... for your father and for you."

Dan Gelber actually did mean it. Anyway, he thought he did, or he wanted to. It was as if he were willing a closeness between them before it would normally happen. He was playing a role. Nevertheless, a hint of a tear appeared in Molly's eye. She looked beautiful in the patio light, Dan thought. He smiled. She blew him a kiss.

"If I may be so bold, monsieur." It was the waiter, finally handing them their menus. They took their time at the Closerie. "You are American tennis player Jay Reynolds?" Dan nodded. "Welcome to Paris. The maître d' ask if you might autograph menu for restaurant. We have collection of famous guests."

"*Avec plaisir.*" Dan took the pen from the waiter. "*Y a-t-il quelque chose que vous voudriez que j'écrive?*"

"Write what you wish, monsieur."

Dan scribbled his best wishes and handed the menu back to the waiter.

"*Merci, monsieur Reynolds, et bonne chance dans le tournoi.* There is much competition."

"*Je vous en pris.*"

"French too?" said Molly, staring at Dan whose accent was almost perfect. "You didn't waste your time on computer games like most teenage boys."

"It's in the guidebook under useful phrases. Zhe-voos-uhn-pree… You're very welcome. Just like the old 'Tell your cab driver 'Sank - roo-" He stopped himself. He really was digging a hole. That was from the an ad in the old Paris Herald Tribune. Did that paper even exist anymore, outside the Godard movie?

He changed the subject quickly back to the foundation. The question was whether to back existing research institutes or perhaps even start one of their own under Molly's direction. She wasn't sure she was ready, but perhaps in a few years. In any case, they decided to go forward with the "I'm Walkin' Foundation," named for a song by rock and roll pioneer Fats Domino, a favorite, Dan explained, of his grandfather who played it himself on the piano when Dan was a toddler. "I'm walkin', yes indeed,/ and I'm talkin' 'bout you and me/I'm hopin' that you'll come back to me."

Dan couldn't get those lyrics out his mind as he warmed up for the finals of the French Open. "What you gonna do when the well runs dry?/You gonna run away and hide/I'm gonna run right by your side/For you pretty baby I'll even die." He had defeated Sasha Zverev, again, in the semis and was now the talk of Paris. Was it conceivable that he could defeat Rafael Nadal, the King of Clay, on the fabled red dirt of Roland Garros where the Spaniard had won an astonishing twelve times? No one had approached that record at a Grand Slam.

Even warming up with Nadal was, Dan Gelber told himself, a unique experience. At the start, Rafa ran out on the court at near top speed as if to demonstrate the superiority of his fitness - something that was almost always true no matter the opponent - before they began. Then he didn't just warm up. He went for blood, hitting with maximum force to intimidate the opposition before the official points even started, using his legendary topspin to make those opponents, even relatively tall ones like Dan at six-two, feel as if they needed to stand on tiptoes just to reach the ball, let alone get it back to the other side with any offensive power. You never knew exactly where Rafa's ball would land either. It flew high off his freshly-strung Babalot as if it were going to land way out, even hit the fence, but then, due to the extraordinary rotation he imparted, the laws of physics would take over, vacuums would be created, and the ball would suddenly dip to land square on the line, only to bound upwards again, this time crashing into that same fence but on the high bounce.

Gelber realized Hicks was right about needing a pogo stick. But he had prepared Dan well. He had shown him video tapes of Djokovic, the one player who had found a way of neutralizing Nadal's high-bounding shots, intercepting them on the way up and rocketing them back as deeply as possible. Dan did just that on his second shot of the warm-up, surprising the Spaniard for a split second before he sent the ball flying back with even more pace, sending a message. Dan felt the reverberations up to his shoulder.

It was shortly thereafter, taking a breather before the match started while swallowing the proscribed two sips of the energy concoction that had been prepared for him, that Dan noticed Dr. Withers and Abelson sitting several rows back in the stands near an entryway. This was the first time he had seen the representatives of the World Anti-Doping Agency at one of his matches. Or at anybody's matches, for that matter. He didn't even know they actually went to matches. He strained to see them against the sun, unsure they were actually there. Had they come because of Nadal or because of him? For years, since well before he began his second life, Dan had heard the gossip that the extraordinarily fit Spaniard used steroids. The accusation made some sense from his then fan's perspective. Rafa's shoulders and arms, that he enjoyed showing off with cut-offs t-shirts, resembled those of an Olympic weight lifter. Either the man was spending 18 hours a day in the gym, or he was taking something. But those rumors never materialized and had now faded away, probably from lack of substance. Meanwhile, ironically, that morning, also for the first time, and because he was in a Grand Slam final, Dan had taken a double dose of Gombo's herbs. Would Withers and Abelson be testing him the minute he walked off court? He was taking a risk.

When play began, he was having a difficult time getting the presence of the two WADA agents out of his mind. After hitting a routine overhead that landed several inches out, he was convinced he caught a glimpse of them out of the corner of his eye, whispering to each other and laughing at him. After another miss, a down the line backhand ruled out by the Hawk-Eye after Dan had protested, Dr. Withers seemed to be wagging her finger at him, almost taunting. How could that be? Was she really doing that? She was a professional. She wasn't supposed to be rooting for or against an individual player.

Before he knew it, he was behind 3-1, the one game being a gift from Nadal on a shanked overhead of his own. Then it was 4-1 and 5-1. Dan was headed for a rout. It looked as if this best of five final was going to be over in an hour. The fans were bored and restless. He heard some booing. Though loyal to Nadal, the long-adopted hometown favorite from umpteen victories on the legendary Court Philippe Chatrier, they wanted at least the semblance of a match for their euros. They wanted this young American phenom to show his stuff. Most of them had even returned early from lunch, breaking the time-honored Roland Garros tradition of always putting *déjeuner* before play - they were French, for god sakes, and must finish all their courses, including wine and cheese, before returning to something so vulgar and ephemeral as an athletic contest.

The first set ended worse than it began, with Dan hitting four straight faults to conclude the matter at 6-1. He had lost the last game at love on his service. Humiliated, he dared not look over at his box where Molly was sitting with her father and the team. Instead, he signaled to the ref he needed a toilet break - you were entitled to two in a five-set match - and ran off with his head bowed down the entryway not far from where Abelson and the doctor were seated. He crashed through the door into the bathroom to find himself alone except for an older man at the urinal. The man, clearly recognizing Jay Reynolds, smiled and Dan nodded back, waiting patiently for him to relieve himself. As soon as the man had washed and gone, Dan reached into his pocket, feeling one of Gombo's pills wrapped in a tissue. He hesitated to take it out, debating, whether this was somehow a defining moment. He was doping in his own way. Or had he already passed the point of no return a long time ago? Equally, was the pair from WADA laying a trap for him? Were exotic, hitherto unknown, at least in the West, Himalayan plants now on the excluded list with meldonium or good, old fashioned steroids? Dan had read there had been little true scientific investigation into ancient herbal medicines because no one could have a patent. There was no money in it. So no one really knew, even about common Ayurvedic remedies like turmeric. Whatever, Dan knew was a certain loser without Gombo's ministrations. The Spaniard was already humiliating him, the ensuing sets would be worse, an epic failure, a disgrace - Dan found himself surprised to be thinking - to his country. To the red, white and blue. Did he really believe that? Was that just some pompous patriotic excuse for his own pain and personal problems he was having so much trouble escaping in his second life? Still, it oddly mirrored some feeling he had been having at the end of his first life. Was he fighting for himself or for others? America hadn't had a Grand Slam winner in years. For Dan Gelber it was almost like that fantasy he had had as a boy – that he was a member of the *lamed vov*, that small group selected to save the world, only in this case the world was the most crucial tennis match of his life.

He swallowed the pill and rushed out onto the court with a determined jog that replicated Nadal who was himself running in place at the opposite end, as if he had never stopped to rest while Dan was hiding out embarrassed in the men's room. It was the Spaniard's serve and, as if to put down a marker for the rest of the match, he rifled a 220km bomber, his fastest of the match, down the T. It exploded off the centerline, generating a cloud of red powder up to Dan's waist, a sure winner if not an ace, but somehow Dan, in one of those rare moments when intense concentration can stretch a split second seemingly into minutes, managed to get his racket on the ball, cutting it short with a sharp flick of the wrist away from his body, catching the outside of the ball and sending it in a slight curve toward the baseline on Nadal's backhand side. The Spaniard sprang for it, but the ball kept veering off, further, further until it simply skittered off the intersection at the precise point the singles and baselines met, a clean, almost magical, winner. Nadal flailed at it helplessly. The cheering crowd rose to its feet. Were they witnessing a miracle? Were they actually going to have a competitive match of all things? As Dan walked over to the ad court to receive the next serve, he glanced up at the section where Abelson and Dr. Withers were seated. They were gone. Replacing them was a single figure with an empty seat beside him. He was dressed all in white and wearing a Panama tilted down over his forehead. Dan squinted into the sun for a better look. It was Gombo. He tipped his hat and nodded. At that moment Dan realized with a certainty that he would win the French Open.

Not that it was that easy. With whatever supernatural help Dan had, his opposition was Rafael Nadal, a supernatural athlete in his own, perhaps more natural, way. After Dan won the second and third sets relatively easily 6-2, 6-3, Rafa came back with a vengeance in the fourth. In the opening game he passed Dan twice on his serve and then engaged him in the longest rally of the match that went thirty-two shots before Nadal hit one of his patented inside out foreheads that not even Usain Bolt could have reached. Dan bent over, gasping for breath. How could Rafa in his thirties with all his injuries - back, knees, elbow, who knows what - have outlasted Dan who was now, in his current avatar, but twenty-two? Was he still carrying around all those extra miles from his previous life along with all the vexing memories? Was he suddenly about to expire when victory was within his grasp, indeed promised to him? Wasn't he supposed to be invincible? He looked up at Gombo who appeared to be unperturbed. He was busy texting someone on his cellphone! Was it Satan? Beelzebub? Shiva? Yen-lo-Wang? Whoever it was, the Nepali was engrossed, as if the game were of little consequence to him. If Gombo wasn't concerned, why should he be? Dan smiled to himself, bounced the ball a few times and sent two aces rocketing past Nadal who still won that second game.

An hour and forty minutes later, however, Dan was walking up the ramp of the makeshift podium to receive the Coupe des Mousquetaires - or at least to hold the original aloft. He would be given a replica later. Dan Gelber had won the French Open. But had he? Was it really he, he wondered, who had won this fabled Grand Slam, the first American to have done so since Agassi in 1999. Or had he, in effect, cheated? Throughout the ceremony, he kept pushing this uncomfortable thought from his mind, but only with moderate success. Did his arrangement with Gombo cheapen his triumph - or worse, invalidate it? Still, he reminded himself it was his inside-out forehead, not Nadal's, that had closed out the tie-breaker and given him a decisive four-set victory. It was he who had deftly side stepped to his left while simultaneously swinging the racket, no Nepalese shaman holding his arm, catching the ball at the precise moment and wrong footing the Spaniard who had been expecting a down the line, inside-in, shot at his weaker backhand. Dan Gelber had done this by himself, he told himself several times, as if to convince himself, and he did this without magic potions. This was his moment, after all, what he had dreamed of since his first times playing tennis in his childhood, hitting balls with his father on those threadbare courts up in the Bronx. The pills he was taking were the next things to placebos, he told himself, over-priced pseudo-scientific nostrums of the type designed to tempt the gullible surfing Amazon for the secret to eternal life or, less monumentally, relief from some minor arthritis pains. They would be about as useful as a pack of M&Ms in defeating Rafael Nadal.

By then Gombo had vanished from the scene and Dan had performed the ritual he had seen so often on television, joyfully climbing over the court fence into the box where his team was waiting, embracing everyone, smooching Molly until they both were gasping for air and giving her father an affectionate, but studiously light punch to the shoulder. Hicks himself had tears in his eyes. He grasped Dan's hands and said a heartfelt "Thank you, my friend. Your courage is amazing. You are a true competitor, your name forever in the history books. You have dethroned the King of Clay." Dan thought of saying "I did it for you. You are the one with the real courage," but the words stuck in his throat. Instead he said a more ambiguous "Thank you," adding "Thank all of you!" for the rest of the team.

That night he went out celebrating with the team. They hit clubs from Le Marais to St. Germain. Everyone seemed to recognize Dan, *le nouveau héro américain*, his face emblazoned on the front of that evening's *France Soir* for the benefit of those few who hadn't seen the match on the television screens that were everywhere in the city. They all drank copious champagne but laid off the cocaine and other drugs on offer. People understood. Dan was in training, after all. Gradually the team peeled off, but Dan and Molly kept going, dancing the night away into the small hours. "Where do you get the energy," said Molly? "This afternoon you played hours of tennis with one of the greatest of all time. And now you're up at five a. m. I can't believe you can even stand."

"You're going home. I want as much time with you as possible." He drew her close. Molly had to be back in San Diego in two days for her orthopedics residency that involved some advanced research. The hospital had given her time off as a special favor for the French Open, but Dan made no effort to ask her to extend and come with him to England, to the Queen's Cup and then to Wimbledon. He had learned in his previous life the danger of asking a woman to give up her career for his. It had been the hidden problem in his first marriage.

Well, maybe not so hidden, even though he would never have overtly asked for such a thing. Before Cynthia quit and became a life counselor, Dan Gelber and his ex were both aspiring writers, something their friends warned was a ticket to disaster. The envy and competition would shatter them. But the young Dan had the publicly avowed values of the time to shield him, he thought, and pledged his allegiance at the beginning of their marriage to the then incipient women's liberation movement. He even went so far as to be among the founders of the first men's consciousness raising group in Los Angeles, formed in response to one of the first women's groups, of which his wife was a member. But both groups soon dissolved after only a few months. There were too many affairs among the members. His ex-wife was even doing it with his best friend, not that Dan himself didn't indulge. Oh, the seventies, he thought - what an everlasting moment of self-delusion they were, almost as bad as the sixties, or maybe worse.

Suddenly an overwhelming feeling of hopelessness came over him.

"What's wrong?" Molly asked.

"Nothing. I'm okay." He cleared his throat and did a little jig.

"I love that dance you taught me - The Hustle. The DJ was blown away."

"Just because I won a tennis match. He would've ignored me otherwise. It's not much of a dance anyway. You can't really go wrong. You just wave your hands around and shake your booty."

"Come on. You had everyone in the club doing it? Where'd you learn it?"

".... On YouTube, where else? ... Want to dance more?" Dan still felt strangely out of body. In his previous life he wasn't much of a dancer. But then he wasn't that much of an athlete either.

"Not now. I want to have your baby. Now, before I have to go back to San Diego."

"But we're not even married yet."

"I'm surprised you're so bourgeois, my love."

"Live and learn."

IX

TENTAZIONE

Dan was introduced to Olga Panova - known as the Second Sharapova or Sharapova Deux, depending on the news outlet, and, at twenty, the only professional female tennis player who doubled as a runway model for five of the world's leading fashion houses - by his son. They were at a garden party given by the Fever-Tree premium tonic people who were sponsoring this year's Queen's Cup, the traditional warm-up for Wimbledon. Ogee, as Olga was called, was six-one and stood about two inches taller than Dan in her four-inch stilettos that, in this instance, were Jimmy Choos. She was, if anything, more extraordinary-looking than Sharapova herself, with a figure that might have been sculpted by Praxiteles, the deepest azure blue eyes and trestles of rust-colored red hair characteristic, he later learned, of her birthplace, the Central Russian province of Udmertia - not that she had spent much time there. She had grown up along Lake Como in a villa owned by her oligarch father somewhere between the residences of George Clooney and Pliny the Younger.

"Jay, I'd like you to meet Ogee," said Zack, trying to suppress a smile. "She's not playing Queens of course. No women. But she'll be at Wimby... Ogee, this is Jay, although I'm sure, like the rest of the world, you know who he is and have seen him play."

"For sure," she said, with only the slightest hint of a Russian accent. Or was it Italian? "I have watched you play many times. What beautiful form. So Gucci!"

Gucci? He hadn't heard that before. The names of fashion houses were the new terms of approbation? You couldn't get more materialistic than that. "Thank you. You're pretty Gucci yourself - a lot more than I am... *for sure.*" That last came out with an automatic smile. He was flirting without even deciding to do it. But, he assumed, she was used to that. Was his son deliberately placing temptation in his way, Dan Gelber wondered. If so, he had learned a lot. Perhaps he had underestimated Zack. "I've seen you on the cover of half the best magazines in the West," Gelber added.

"Don't throw shade on Asia, snack." She pretended to frown in a playful way. "Their magazines are dank."

"You would know. I'm sure you're on the covers." Dank? Snack? He could hardly keep up with the slang. How long was it since he had been to Brooklyn? Or maybe he should have been hanging out on Instagram. The way she looked, she must have had about fifty million followers. Still, he suspected all the argot was a bit of a put on. This young lady was clearly what his grandmother would have called "to the manor born." The words seemed like they came from some list of the latest trendy slang you might find on the Facebook page for Teen Vogue, but what did he know?

"Unfortunately, I cannot read their interviews. Perhaps they do not like me."

"I would doubt that. It doesn't seem possible."

Dan Gelber did his best to appear relaxed, but underneath was feeling more than a little bit overwhelmed, as if he were interacting with the most popular girl in his high school class, the one he would never have dared asked out to avoid rejection - although, as he later learned, these same girls often sat home alone on Saturday night.

"Well," said Zack, "now that we have this, uh, mutual admiration society going, Ogee, perhaps you can get Jay to do what I've been bothering him about for months.... sign up with Nike."

"You do not like Nike?" said Ogee with half-serious smile. "Is great global brand – and I am sure they give you excellent contract."

."I'm sure they would. But I like to buy my own clothes."

"Really? That can get bougee."

"For shorts and a t-shirt?" He pretty well got what bougee meant, but the twinkle in her eye now convinced him it was all a put-on.

"I think they would give you more than just shorts and t-shirts. Perhaps your own Bentley and house on Riviera."

"I wouldn't go that far," said Zack. "But who knows? Win Wimbledon and the sky is yours.... I'm going to leave you two and try to hustle some lesser players. Great going, champ. Roland Garros - amazing! Sampras couldn't even do that.... Next up - a designer line like Federer. The Reynolds Hoodie. Ask Ogee - she knows all about that."

He clapped Dan on the back and headed off.

Dan Gelber had quite deliberately and successfully been avoiding Zack since Indian Wells - being in business with his own son under these circumstances would have been by several degrees too weird for Gelber - but he had trumped him this time with Ogee. He had indeed underestimated him.

"Zack really wants to land you," Ogee continued. "He would go to the top of Nike for that. You should let him. He's nice boy... like you," she added with a smile, taking his arm. "I even see resemblance... not physically, of course, but something in your style... Shall we get some champagne?"

"I'm not sure I should."

"You are not thirsty?" She dragged out the last ward to give it at least six meanings.

Who wouldn't be, he was about to say, but stopped himself. "Look, Ogee, I have to tell you something.... You're magnificent and in another life... or in this life... or the next one... I can't figure out which one but never mind... I'd be pursuing you all over the galaxy, but I'm engaged."

"I know that, silly. Everybody does. Relax and have fun."

Dan Gelber did what she said, to the extent he could, and they had a couple of glasses of Dom Perignon. And then another two. Soon Dan was relaxing his guard. Almost without realizing he was doing it, he started telling Ogee about a trip to Russia he had in his previous life. Actually, it was one of several. He had gone twice in Soviet times on "cultural exchanges."

"You were invited to a film festival in Siberia?" she said.

"Yes. A few years ago. The friend who called me told me it was my chance to go to Siberia and to come back? Dark Russian humor, I suppose."

Ogee stared at him. "How old were you? Fifteen?"

"Er, yeah. Something like that.... It was a children's film festival.... Teen films. They wanted an American. Disney and all that."

"And you went by yourself? That's cool."

"You mean dank." She laughed. They looked at each other for a moment. "Actually, it was an incredible experience," Dan continued, slightly nervous. "Got to see the Northern Lights. The taiga - the vast expanse of snow. They even took me in a helicopter over the Gulag… to see where Trotsky had been in prison." Now he had gone too far - even though it was the truth.

"My father says Trotsky was not good man, although some in West love him."

"Your father's right. I used to feel that way too but… then I grew up." Now she was really staring at him. It was definitely time to change the subject. "So, uh, how do you like your draw at Wimbledon?"

"Not so much. I play Azarenka in second round and Venus in third if I get through."

"Venus is a force of nature, isn't she?"

"She is… You know, Jay, you are interesting person. Most Americans know little of Russia except Putin and vodka, but you seem to have great knowledge - and you are only two years older than me. I am impressed…I think …" She touched him gently on the sleeve. "…we should perhaps get to know each other better. Maybe hang out."

Dan exhaled slowly, having a pretty good idea of what hanging out entailed.

He was reminded of that when he double-faulted at deuce in the very first game of his first match at the All England Club. Just as he tossed the ball for the serve, he noticed Ogee sliding into the second row behind the royal box. It was devoid of royals at that point - that would come later when, starting with the round of sixteen, Prince Harry and Meghan Markle, aka the Duchess of Sussex, attended his every match. Although he had never cared for her in his previous life,the American Meghan was apparently rooting for Jay for nostalgic patriotic reasons. Whatever the case, she was nowhere in Ogee's league. Dan wasn't the only one who noticed the tennis playing runway idol, of course, at that moment, though the only one who would lose a point because of it. He made it up quickly, however, winning his first round that was actually his second round because, as the fourth seed, he was given a bye, in straights 3, 2, and 2.

Even in the required Wimbledon whites Ogee stood out among all women at center court. To the annoyance of some other players, Dan would contest all his matches on that legendary court during the tournament. He was, the British acknowledged, a sensation no one wanted to miss. She was accompanied by a short, squat man wearing a Dolce & Gabbana leather baseball hat and purple suspenders Dan correctly suspected was her father. The two of them were there each time he played.

Every night he was on the phone with Molly, FaceTime across nine time zones.

"You're sure you don't want me to come? It's your first Wimbledon," she said more than once.

"Aren't you working on that new tech with that doctor from Tel Aviv?"

"Dr. Itzig. Dr. Patel from Mumbai is here too. The two most important men in robotic exoskeletons in the world. It's amazing what they do, turning so many lives around."

"More important than any tennis game."

Molly went silent. How could she deny it?

"It's okay. You can be with me at the US Open in September."

"Yes, my love. And I can always see you online in the Daily Mail," she added with a laugh. "They cover your every move now as if you were a Kardashian. I saw you at Kensington Palace with that model Ogee whatever's-her-name?"

"Panova."

"She's gorgeous. If you had an affair with her, I wouldn't blame you."

"Yes, you would. And I'd blame myself."

"Well, that's nice to hear because...." She went silent again.

"Because what?"

"Because I think I'm pregnant.... Actually, I am pregnant."

"Wow!" Dan FaceTimed excitedly. So soon? He was skeptical he could even have a child this time - Gombo had said nothing about it and he hadn't asked - but maybe he was even more fertile in his second life. Or Molly was. What would the child be like? Would he or she have some kind of miraculous powers? No, that was ridiculous. "This is great news. When do you want to get married? I don't want to be one of those trendy idiots who has six kids and never marries because they can't commit or something... "

"Or it's too bourgeois."

"I'll never be a hipster, I guess. Not in this life. I had enough of that."

"What?"

"Nothing.... Look, I don't want to interrupt your research or anything - it's crucial - but.... we should make plans, no?"

"I know. I have to admit I've been looking at your tournament schedule. There's a two-week gap right after the Open."

"Perfect. Where should we do it?"

By this time, he was in the quarterfinals at Wimbledon. It had been the proverbial whirlwind - endless press conferences and photoshoots. Interviews with Martina Navratilova and Paul Annacone. Dinners with Jim Courier who signed him up for the US Davis Cup team. "Where've you been all these years?" "I'm only twenty-two." "We needed you when you were fifteen." Two days later he was winning his semi against Del Potro in straight sets. The big moment loomed. Mano-a-mano against Roger Federer, arguably the most famous athlete on the planet with the exception of some soccer players few in America had ever heard of and maybe LeBron James. But it was Federer who had lasted longer at number one and he had done it by itself, with no assists from team members, as if he were a prize fighter who ruled the world for an unheard-of decade and a half. If there was anyone who had transcended time, it was Roger. He didn't need a second life. His first one would suffice.

Ironically, Dan Gelber had met the great Federer before, although he was certain Roger wouldn't remember. How could he? It was during Dan's previous life. He was driving up to the Hancock Tennis Club not more than a month before his operation to practice for the seniors' final he never played when he discovered a film crew had taken over the parking lot. He had to park some blocks away and walk up. The receptionist told him the crew was there filming a Mercedes commercial on Court Two with Roger Federer. They were almost finished but if Dan hurried, he might catch a glimpse of the great man.

Unlike most of his tennis player peers, Dan was never much of a Federer fan. The man was too perfect, almost inhumanly so. He had everything and never made a mistake in public or in private, as far as Dan Gelber knew. He could win Grand Slams without mussing up his hair and then, in the press conference, graciously praise his opponents in one of who-knew-how-many languages, while an admiring world gasped and applauded. How could he do this for so long? He was rewriting the physical longevity code for Homo Sapiens and saving Africa at the same time. He was a God among men, as much as anyone alive, and Dan, ever the contrarian, resented him. So he decided, at that particular moment, he wouldn't bother to watch Federer flacking the pleasures of luxury German automobiles and instead go practice his own most unFedererer-like serve on one of the back courts when he ran straight into the man himself who, naturally and graciously extended his hand to the aging seventy-something plebeian in his tennis togs, saying, out of nowhere, "Nice to see you. You have a terrific club here," as if they were intended to have a real relationship of some kind. Or was he as much a politician as a legendary athlete? Dan could do nothing but stammer a "thank you," though he had nothing to do with the club's attractions pro or con, as Federer gave him a friendly clap on the shoulder and went on his way.

Indeed, Dan Gelber had a sufficient level of introspection to realize his view of the exceptionally accomplished like Roger Federer had always been a complicated one, distorted by a complex cocktail of admiration and envy. When working in Hollywood, he had frequently felt diminished, even a bit angry, when in the presence of revered directors of the Scorsese or Spielberg ilk, as if he, Dan Gelber, were somehow therefore deficient, not just as an artist, but as a human being, and should be judged accordingly. His life would be irrelevant. Yet here he was rallying with the man thought of by many to be the greatest ever to play the game of tennis on Wimbledon center court, the cathedral of tennis, warming up for the finals. Surreal was far too weak a term. It wasn't the first time he felt he was having an out-of-body experience, but it certainly was the furthest out one of all. He was playing in the finals of the most famous tennis tournament, arguably one of the most celebrated sporting events of any sort in the world, particularly for solo practitioners, against its most legendary competitor. He would have stopped to pinch himself but the balls were flying so fast it was out of the question.

To settle himself, he glanced over at Molly in his box. She smiled, although she didn't realize what he was thinking. How could she? Two nights before, after the semis, she had called him and told him she was getting on a plane. She couldn't miss him in the finals.

"Don't bother," he said. "It's Federer at Wimbledon. I don't stand a chance."

"Suddenly modest? I thought we were going to have a foundation. Besides, my father says you're going to win."

"That's not what he tells me."

"He's trying to prepare you for a match. He'll say what he has to."

"But what about those doctors from everywhere?"

"They'll live without me for a day."

So she came. And he was glad, relieved really, even though she would be returning to California the next morning at the crack of dawn, a dizzying roundtrip across North America and the Pond all in thirty-six hours. She assured him the tiny fetus in her womb wouldn't notice. She was sitting in the box with his team, not far from the Duke and Duchess of Cambridge who were seated with Theresa May and across from actors Hugh Grant, Eddie Redmayne and Benedict Cumberbatch. They were just down from the ubiquitous Sir Elton John, almost as much a symbol of his country as the Queen. London mayor Sadiq Khan sat only a row further back, not far from Ogee and her father who, in turn, were just behind a row of former Wimbledon standouts - Stefan Edberg, Chrissie Evert and Bjorn Borg. He also recognized soccer star David Beckham and his designer wife Victoria, all come to see him. Or was it Federer? Of course, it was Federer. How could it be otherwise? But he did have an opponent and that was Dan. And he knew that was only the beginning of the celebrities and billionaires who had paid God knew how much for something called debenture seats that sounded more like bonds or securities than they did admissions to a sports event. And maybe that's what they were. Out of body experience indeed.

Nevertheless, defeating Federer was surprisingly easy that day. Dan did it in straight sets without going to a tie-breaker once. The Swiss's legendary serve was there, but somehow Dan was able to read it, knew preternaturally which way was it was going - left or right with the occasional body serve - and took the returns early, rocketing them back at an increasingly befuddled Federer's feet. He was also able to dip down low on Federer's sliced backhand, slicing it back himself A couple of times he even stole his opponent's surprise trick of charging forward during the service toss in the pattern known as the SABR - "Sneak Attack By Roger" - the second time causing Federer to smash his racquet on the sacred Center Court turf, breaking it apart and earning a penalty. The crowd seemed agitated by this uncharacteristic behavior from the saint of the sport.

Dan didn't take pleasure in that even though in the decades-long Federer-Nadal-Djokovic competition Dan, unlike most fans, had always preferred the Serb for his antic sense of humor. And in the third set, after Federer got another penalty, this time - incredibly - for a foot fault (he was usually so meticulous) and was deducted a point, knowing he had an unseen advantage, Dan almost dialed back his play. Roger must have finally, at 37, been getting old or, as Lawrence of Arabia might have said of Dan's victory, "It was written," except he noted with a smile, remembering one of his favorite films, that Lawrence had actually responded to the little Arab boys that "Nothing is written." Any man could do anything if he had sufficient courage matched with that infinite capacity for greatness that lurks in some of us, waiting to be tapped. At least that was the way it was in the movie. Of course, neither T. E. Lawrence, nor writer Robert Bolt nor director David Lean knew anything of Gombo or his herbs or what they could accomplish. A new life, a better life. The Nepali was not in attendance for the Wimbledon final, as far as Dan could tell. Maybe at this point he didn't need to be. Jay Reynolds' tennis abilities could stand on their own. Some, on the fan websites, were already speaking of him as a potential GOAT, the greatest of all time, an honor debated almost exclusively among that same trio Federer, Nadal and Djokovic with an occasional nod to Rod Laver, a seemingly obligatory bow to the sports' past when the game was considerably slower and less athletic, more a country club activity for the upper classes, though there were outliers. Fred Perry, the first to win a career Grand Slam, had emerged in the 1930s from the slums of East London.

Those Fred Perry roots were a distant memory, however, when, hours later, Dan clutched the trophy, parading about the posh environs of the Fifteenth Century Guild Hall, its large medieval crypts repurposed for such glamorous events as the Wimbledon Championship Party. Dan had felt a twinge as he kissed Molly good-bye, a thousand cameras catching the moment, on her departure to the airport. But now he was dancing the ceremonial waltz with the women's winner, Simona Halep of Romania. For once almost childlike, he wished that his parents could have been there to see him, but then he recalled he had no parents or was supposed to have none in this life. He was an orphan. And in his real life, if you could call it that, his father had had an ambivalent attitude to Dan's successes (wasn't that true of many fathers), over-excited when he won a minor literary prize in his twenties and then rushing home to write a novel of his own when, as far as the young Dan knew, he had never dreamed of doing such a thing. Dan quietly rejoiced when the first few pages were terrible. His father ultimately abandoned the task.

What would he have made of a success on this level? Sports, as it so often was, had been an area of simultaneous learning and competition between father and son. His father, a distinguished surgeon but only a so-so athlete, had been the one who had introduced him to tennis, a game then for those too small for basketball or football. Surprisingly, by the age of twelve Dan was beating him occasionally and his father soon declined to play. A few years later, however, he turned up for a high school jayvee match at which Dan was losing, all the more so because his father was present. At the finish, his father compared his play to his victorious opponent who he said had admirable "conservation of motion." That was his father's mantra about sports, conservation of motion was the ticket to greatness, like Joe DiMaggio or Rocket Laver. Dan should try to do that, though Dan knew the subtext was 'you never will.' You'll never be good enough. You'll never be a real man. At least it wasn't Oedipus Rex. When, decades later, across time and space, he attended the post-Oscar's Governor's Ball, seated far from the dais, almost in another room if that were possible, where they put screenwriters, merely an Academy Award nominee but still something impressive for a moment, the career pinnacle of his previous life actually, his father was already dead.

"Jay... you are amazing player... most amazing I have seen..." It was Simona Halep, blurting out suddenly sotto voce for the benefit of all in the Guild Hall at the conclusion of their ceremonial dance. "It is historical."

The tony crowd of lords, ladies, celebrities and athletes applauded or murmured their agreement.

"No, no... really. I just got lucky. This won't last. Someone in the Big Three... or maybe even Murray ... that should make this country happy... or one of the younger players, Khachanov or Zverev ... will win the US Open and everything will be back to normal.... I promise," he added with what he hoped would appear a humble smile. He certainly felt that way - or wanted to. It was more confusing than he expected. Where was Molly? Oh, gone already.

"Lucky? I have never seen anything like your play. Not even Novak in 2011." Halep added in perfect Eastern European accented English. Where did all these tennis players get their language skills? "You will change our sport. We are all watching you now. You are the new God. Congratulations!" The Romanian bowed her head deferentially as the music resumed again. That last had made Dan dizzy. It was too much.

"May I cut in?" It was Ogee.

X

THE LOCKER ROOM

Like most lifelong sports fans, Dan Gelber had for years heard about the importance of the locker room. It was the place where mutual respect was built among the players, where men revealed themselves to each other in their nakedness, not so much about the obvious - the extent of their endowments - but about who they were, the attractiveness of their personalities. Was this someone they could live with or, in the case of an individual sport like tennis, someone they would enjoy spending time with, despite, or even because of, the constant competition between them, as the caravan moved across the globe? Being popular in the locker room was coveted—not as much, of course, as victory on the court, but enough—especially by Gelber who, in his first life, rarely felt he was considered a desired comrade. In a sense he was correct in that. Although not a complete loner, he tended to be standoffish. This was interpreted by some as arrogance but was in many ways the reverse, a feeling of inferiority, of not being up to snuff athletically and, although he didn't like to admit it, socially or even professionally. As a resident of Hollywood, California, he had been conditioned into the pervasive local belief that his credits were him—or, as was said locally, you were only as good as your last picture, a sure fire recipe for perpetual emotional dysfunction.

Thus Gelber, as a man of his time and place, often struggled with self-acceptance, He wanted to, in the very parlance he often ridiculed, self-actualize. It was an ambiguous term with myriad definitions, but what it came down to was being the popular kid he had never been in high school. He recognized his tremendous success in his new life as an opportunity to achieve this. They were the film credits he had never had. He also realized that might be a naive, even immature view, but who wouldn't want to be revered like Federer, he thought in the end, to be an international symbol of both sporting and human perfection? It was the apotheosis of the life well lived, even if some disdained it as shallow. Did they have a right to, he wondered? It was easy enough to be holier than thou. Others had been down the same road, he knew. When he was young and first winning important tournaments, Djokovic had used comedy, an extraordinary ability to mimic other players, male and female, to ingratiate himself with his colleagues. The Serb's results from this approach had been mixed, some finding him charming but others dismissing him as childish and overly needy of approval. But even if Gelber could improve on this, he had no such comic gift, nor did Jay Reynolds who was, as yet, a person and personality in formation, still in his chrysalis form despite his formidable down-the-line backhand and unreturnable serve down the T. He would have to rely on the force of his will, which sometimes translated as false bonhomie or over eagerness and left others puzzled. The natural jealousy toward an overly successful newcomer only exacerbated the matter. Try as he might, Gelber was not relaxed in the locker room, especially in close proximity to those he had formally regarded as gods, or at least near gods. He was as yet to get the camaraderie he sought.

Hicks sensed this. The coach was well-received, even sought after in the room in part due to sympathy for his infirmity but also from knowledge accrued from years of watching others while being unable to play. He knew how to handle himself and others in most situations. He also knew that, for the long run, it was advisable Jay Reynolds should be more comfortable with his peers. He would have to deal with them for a lot of years and they with him. When, about a month after Wimbledon, he saw Dan, whom he of course knew as Jay, sitting not far from Federer though still not able to engage in anything resembling a casual conversation, Hicks decided to take Jay aside for a discreet player-coach pep talk.

The wheelchair-bound man often gave him useful advice. Early on, before his first major tournament, he told Jay that the trick to dealing with the immense pressure that was to come was to love it rather than fear it. "Pressure is your friend," he said. "Take advantage of it. Embrace it." This time he said: "Stop acting guilty when you're around Roger. He's a man, like you. Not Christ on the cross. You won, he lost. That happens. Play him again and it'll be other way around. In fact, I promise you it will if you keep signaling you did something wrong. He'll see that in a second and you'll pay for it."

"I'll make an effort," Gelber said, although it was oddly unnerving with Federer since he had met the maestro by accident that day in his previous life. He sometimes wondered if Roger would recognize him, extremely unlikely as that would be, almost impossible.

"You'll be glad you did," Hicks replied. "You're part of a business now. They're your colleagues. Remember, this isn't forever. By the time you're in your thirties you'll be finished. Make friends and you'll thrive after that... be a broadcaster... maybe even be a coach," he added with a grin that suddenly morphed into a grimace as he contracted in his chair. Something was wrong with Hicks, some holdover from his accident that never healed.

"Are you okay?"

"Fine, fine.... It's nothing really... I have to shift position every once in a while." Hicks glanced at Gelber who still looked concerned. "Don't worry about it," he continued, sitting up straight and trying to smile with some success. "It's no problem really... I... uh... I never thanked you for the foundation. You didn't have to do that."

"What else should I do with my money? There's nothing better." Gelber didn't like the sound of that. He felt strange, inauthentic. "It's really because of your daughter."

"Yes, she never seems to have gotten over my accident. Neither has my wife."

"...And you?"

"It was difficult at first, but I'm okay with it now."

"Do you... I hope you don't mind my asking but... are you sure it was an accident? Molly said your wife—"

"Yes. I know she wants to believe that. I don't blame her. She had more to deal with than I did. My recovery was long. I couldn't do anything for myself. But it was... what it was. An accident, no more, no less. The semi knocked me clear off the road. My car turned over twice and I was in a coma for weeks. It was a miracle I lived. But here I am. You know the old expression - God works in mysterious ways. Anyway... now I get to live through you. That's more fun. Maybe you can win all four slams at once—

like Djokovic." He smiled again, looked down at his watch. "Time for the weight room, amigo."

Later, after his work out, Gelber went back into the locker room for a shower. Marin Cilic, one of the more friendly players on the tour, was toweling off. "Look who is here" he said playfully in his relatively mild Croatian accent. "Superman…. Remind me never be on your side of draw rest of year."

"That makes two of us, Marin," Gelber replied, opening the door of an empty shower stall.

"Heard you sign with Nike. Not bad."

"Where'd you hear that?"

"Saw their rep last week. Zack something."

"Zack Gelber. It's not true."

"Then I take contract," said Cilic with a grin "I need extra Porsche for beach house. Maybe yacht."

"Go for it, dude."

Dan Gelber stepped inside the stall, closing the door behind him. What was that about, he wondered? Was his son that desperate for a deal he was going around saying he had one even when he didn't? Gelber found the intertwining of his two lives distressing, to say the least. Yet he didn't seem able to escape it. Well, Zack did have his reasons. He had his family to think about, little Peter and his problems. Gelber turned on the shower, letting the water stream down on him, first too cold, then too hot, then, with an adjustment, just right. He stood there with his face turned up to the head, letting the water splash down over his sweaty body, when the sounds started to come again, the crackling nose, louder than ever, with someone yelling "Get out! Get out!" at the top of his lungs. Couldn't anyone else hear this? What was going on?

XI
THERAPY

"Good morning, Mr. Reynolds. How're you feeling today?"

"Not so hot, Dr. Silvera. I wish I could say otherwise, but I'm much the same."

"Still having those dreams...."

"They don't feel like it. They're more real than that. I keep hearing them after I wake up in the middle of the night. They won't go away."

"Someone yelling 'Get out! Get out!'?"

"Yes. And the crackling sound."

"I can understand this must be disturbing for you."

"It is - to say the least. Sometimes I almost feel like I'm going mad. I'd do anything to make it go away."

"You said last time.... How does your wife feel?"

"She's supportive, but she's worried. She's a doctor, as I told you."

"Yes, an orthopedist. She wants to help her father who had a terrible accident. Sounds like a wonderful woman."

"She is. She's beautiful and brilliant. I'm very lucky to be with her - more than you can imagine." That was certainly true. But Gelber wondered for a second if the doctor had seen the photos in the *Daily Mail*, the ones showing him with Ogee Panova at that night club in Monte Carlo. They weren't alone. They were in a group of other tennis players, but the pictures were cropped to make it look as if they were a couple, with accompanying boilerplate implying they might be having an affair. They weren't—not that

Gelber hadn't thought of it. Who wouldn't? Molly was half the world away at the time. Still, he was able to resist. In fact, he felt a little smug about it. Of course, it went without saying that he had a secret he kept from his wife that was far greater than any affair could be, but Dan Gelber didn't want to go there. He didn't want to think about that, not then, not ever. And he certainly didn't want to explain it to the doctor who wouldn't believe it anyway. All he wanted was to get rid of those blasted voices. In his first life, a man of his generation, he had occasionally seen therapists, but ultimately wasn't sure they were actually helpful and wondered if he had wasted his time and money. But maybe this time, just maybe, it was worth a shot. Maybe Silvera, who had come highly recommended, could liberate him. And the doctor had even been a college tennis player himself, at UCLA, but nowhere on the level of Jay Reynolds. There weren't too many who could say that, less than half a dozen in the world, if that.

"My wife was relieved when I told her I was coming to see you," he told Silvera who nodded.

"What do you think it means? The voice telling you to get out... Get out of what?"

"I wish I knew."

"Why don't you take a guess?"

"You mean free associate?"

"If you want to call it that."

"Get out of tennis?"

"Well, that's an interesting choice, considering how well you are doing. Why do you think you... free associated that? We don't use that term so much anymore. But go ahead."

"I think I'm guilty about my success."

"Why is that?"

"I don't feel like I deserve it."

"Why not? You've defeated some of the greatest players of all time... and on several occasions. I saw you on ESPN defeating Federer and Nadal back-to-back. That can't be a fluke. Some are even talking of you being The Goat."

"An exaggeration."

Silvera frowned "Your guilt is indeed extreme, as you no doubt realize."

"Is that why I'm hearing the voices, the crackling? They have to stop. That's why I'm here."

"As you told me."

"There is something else.... I guess I should say."

"Yes?"

The psychiatrist looked at Dan Gelber who hesitated. He clearly wanted to say something, but for Gelber it would have been crossing a personal Rubicon and he wasn't sure it was advisable. In fact, it could be outright dangerous to his life if it were misconstrued. And yet that was why he was here, why he was in therapy. Indeed, he had a strong compulsion to tell and had almost said something in their previous session. Someone had to hear it, after all, and he was in the safety of a doctor's office. How else would he free himself from his demons and hope to go on and live a full life with his family?

"I'm haunted by... guess you would call it... a past life of some sort. I know it sounds crazy but I'm not really... or not exclusively... Jay Reynolds. Sometimes I'm convinced I am.... or was or something... this writer Dan Gelber and that in reality I'm actually approaching my seventy-fifth birthday. I was given a second life by this Nepalese shaman Gombo in the San Fernando Valley."

"And how'd he do that?" The psychiatrist measured his words.

"By giving me Himalayan herbs. They made me younger and we went to Nepal together and engineered my death on Everest. I came back as Jay Reynolds, the twenty-year old tennis phenomenon."

"Like Faust?"

"More or less."

"And where is this Gombo now?"

"I don't know. It's mysterious. He comes and goes. He helps me when I'm in trouble, but he's mercurial. Sometimes I think he's out to get me."

"Like Mephistopheles."

"I suppose."

"And how would he 'get you'?"

"There are a limited number of herbs. He controls that."

"I see."

Silvera sat there a moment. It was, of course, a great deal to digest.

"You must think I'm making this all up. I doubt you believe in past life regression the way people did in the seventies," said Gelber, nodding up at the Yale Medical School diploma on the wall.

"The seventies?" The doctor repeated, as if rolling around the notion in his brain. "Have you told your wife about this?"

"No. Of course not," said Gelber, alarmed.

The doctor waited an even longer time to respond. "This is not an easy situation," he said finally. "The level of your guilt is significant, beyond what I had previously thought. It may be related to the fact that your parents died when you were two and you survived them. I don't know. It's too early to tell." The doctor exhaled. It was clear he was a bit frustrated. "Since, as you have told me, you are leaving for the Australian Open in a few days and then are going on to Dubai for another tournament, who knows when we will see each other again? So, I will break the rules of my profession and tell you straight out you are suffering from what is known as a dissociative identity disorder, popularly called split personality, but that is inaccurate. It is a serious matter and not easily solved. If you don't deal with it, bad... even grave... outcomes may occur for you and those close to you. I am sorry to tell you this, but it is to impress upon you the urgency of your situation. I would highly recommend, while you are in Melbourne, that we stay in close touch via Skype, perhaps with daily sessions, if that can be arranged between your matches."

Dan Gelber nodded, as if signaling his agreement to the doctor. But the reverse had actually occurred. He had finally confessed his greatest secret to someone and felt miraculously liberated. Although Jewish, for a second he imagined himself a Catholic emerging from the confession booth. He had said ten Hail Marys to the psychiatrist and was free to go on with his life. He knew he would never see, or even talk to, Silvera again.

XII

SOME YEARS LATER

"That's you, daddy! On the radio."

"It is. Let's change the channel. Hear some music."

"But he said you were gonna break Federer's record. Win more Slams."

"So big deal." Dan always tried to make light of his success to his four-year old son. He didn't want to burden the boy with it. He often worried the child was surrounded by too much, a home in North San Diego country with three tennis courts (hard court, grass and red clay to practice for Roland Garros), an Olympic pool, its own helipad and landing strip, security detail always around, making sure no family members, including his two-year old sister, were kidnapped. And then there were the vacation homes, the beachfront place in the Virgin Islands and the villa in Cortina d'Ampezzo. "You know, Lucas, I don't think being a pro athlete is really such a great thing. You get to a certain point... maybe in your thirties... I know that seems a long way away to you now, but it really isn't... life's funny that way. I can promise you... But you might... and I know it's a little premature... a lot premature actually.... want to consider a career that lasts a bit longer - a doctor like your mother, or a lawyer, something like that. Even a writer of books. I wanted to do that, believe it or not?"

"You did?" The boy looked wide-eyed.

"You like books. People write books when they're really old."

"Like forty?"

"Even then."

"Why don't you write books, daddy? When you're old."

"I don't think I could… anymore," he replied, purposefully mumbling the last word. They were driving along the Pacific Coast Highway headed for Lucas' favorite frozen yogurt stand. Often at times like this he thought of what Gombo had told him about his longevity, how the herb, in Gombo's experience, didn't last forever, that at some point, often sooner than expected, it wore off or lost potency from over use much like an antibiotic. If that happened, they would have to find a purer strain that might not currently be available even in the Himalayas. Dan had asked the Nepali where that might be, but the shaman was evasive. He told Dan that if he wanted to guard against this rapid aging that could come at any time, he would have to be committed. When Gelber asked what that meant, he was again equivocal. You will know when you need to, he said with a frustrating opaqueness.

Which left Dan to wonder how Lucas would react when and if that process started to happen, when his father began to look like his grandfather or even great grandfather and possibly even died young or youngish, at least in calendar years if not in appearance? How old would Lucas be then? Eleven? Thirteen? Should he be preparing the boy for that or his sister Olivia? No, she was too young for that. He had talked around the subject to Molly, trying to tell her in his way, but afraid to go through with it. What, he asked her once, would she do if she had to be a widow for fifty years? He hoped she would find a new mate. Molly couldn't figure out what he was asking? Was he planning on suicide? She hoped not, at least not before the US Open that would be his seventeenth Grand Slam, growing ever closer to Federer's twenty, and then twenty-one, the generally agreed landmark to be declared the GOAT.

Actually, he would already have reached seventeen, but deliberately lost to Djokovic in the semis of the Australian Open. It didn't raise too many eyebrows, particularly since it was the Serb's signature tournament, where he had won his first slam and had subsequently been victorious more than any other player. No one would notice if Dan couldn't quite reach far enough to his right to return Djokovic's patented two-hander down the line. Few others could. A few weeks later he lost to the young Greek phenom Tsitsipas in the finals of Indian Wells, creating rumors that Jay Reynolds' meteoric rise might be over or that he might have been injured, until he regained form only two months later by winning the French Open yet again.

He had adopted this clandestine defeatist strategy for several reasons but predominantly because Dr. Withers had suddenly taken a greater interest in him. Indeed, she had become something of an Inspector Javert, pursuing him literally everywhere he went. Over the previous two years Dan must have had thirty surprise drug tests, always with Dr. Withers accompanied at various times by different physicians and clinicians.

It had started to get serious at the US Open the year before. "You know, Mr. Reynolds, you have the most extreme case of sports anemia I have ever seen."

"Shouldn't you be calling me Jay by this point, doctor, and what's sports anemia?" They were standing in Dan's recently purchased apartment in the Dakota. It was two floors above the one owned by John and Yoko and had a panoramic view of Central Park.

"A misnomer. It's not really anemia. Athletes tend to have lower hemoglobin concentrations than normal people, even those who jog or work out. Yours are the lowest we've seen."

"Ever seen," said the man beside her who had been introduced as a hematologist from Bellevue Hospital. "Almost otherworldly. If you don't mind, we'd like you to come in for a work-up."

"Does that mean drawing a lot of blood? As you know, I'm in the middle of the Open. I don't want to be collapsing on the court."

"There are anomalies in your previous tests."

"Anomalies? … If that's all it is, we should probably wait. I'm not good with these things. When I gave to a blood drive a few years ago I nearly passed out."

"We only need a few drops to test. Hardly more than a pin prick. And a few other things, scans mainly, that are entirely non-interventionist…. If you like, consider it your contribution to medical science."

The hematologist exchanged a brief look with Dr. Withers as if his last statement had been pre-arranged when Dan's son came into the room. "Daddy, you promised to play Jurassic World Monopoly with me."

"My day off," Dan said to the doctors, jumping at the opportunity.

"Unfortunately, your daddy is busy this afternoon with some requirements," said Dr. Withers and turned to Dan. "I am sorry, Mr. Reynolds, but you must come with us now to avoid the possibility of a suspension."

"A suspension? By whom?"

"Do you want me to say in front of the boy? ... WADA, of course," she added in a lower voice.

"You can't suspend me. I haven't done anything." Dan glanced down at Lucas who was looking more than a little apprehensive that something bad was happening to his father, though it was certain the acronym for the World Anti-Doping Association meant nothing to him. Indeed, it just added to the confusion. It sounded almost like baby talk. Wada-wada.

The work-up took seven hours. Dan couldn't remember having undergone such a battery of tests, not even that fateful time when his back went into spams before the finals of the seniors' tournament or some years before that when he was sure he had a coronary and was brought to the emergency room at two in the morning only to find out it was gall stones.

Dan thought the ordeal would never end, as he was wheeled in a chair down endless hospital corridors as if he were a paraplegic and not a world class athlete, for test after test. It was Western medicine looking for the secrets of Eastern medicine. The longer it went on, the more he was convinced they would find something. At the conclusion, after his teeth were x-rayed in three dimensions and he had a cardiac MRI as well as a brain scan, he was delivered back to the Dakota in a limousine courtesy of WADA without a word from Dr. Withers or the hematologist. "What were they looking for all this time?" Molly asked. "Beats me," Dan replied, rapidly changing the subject to say he had to look at the tapes her father had given of him of his first opponent at the Open, a lucky loser from Cyprus who had made it to the second round into which Dan, as first seed, had the usual bye.

Dan won that tournament, defeating Denis Shapovalov in the final. He allowed the once precocious Canadian to take the third set for similar reasons he had discretely thrown matches to Djokovic and Tsitsipas. Now more than ever he didn't want to raise suspicions. Indeed, he blew that set by focusing his mind during play as much as possible on that day of testing at Bellevue. What were all those machines? He tried to enumerate them to himself. In some cases, it was impossible to tell what they were meant to determine, but they were certainly expensive. He had yet to see the results and wondered if he ever would. Meanwhile, he would scan the stadium for Dr. Withers and one of the WADA representatives but was never able to pick them out. Of course, Arthur Ashe Stadium was so big it would have been easy to miss them.

Dan's preoccupation remained through the rest of the season and on into the next. His supply of pills from Gombo was dwindling and, to preserve them, he took them less often, but it didn't seem to make a difference. Winning came just as easily. And yet, something was disturbing him. He didn't feel exactly the same. Was he slowing down? Aging despite all? He found himself playing tennis more strategically and less physically, relying on gamesmanship. Sometimes he would end points early, go for quick winners rather than commit to painstaking rallies intended to wear his opponents down as he had before. He did this to conserve energy, a technique he had seen Federer use as the maestro moved into his late thirties.

Yet there was more. It seemed to Dan, although he had no way of knowing for sure, that his hands were slowly beginning to look older again. Some days he thought he saw more wrinkles on the back sides, not the way they were when he was seventy in his previous life, but more like forty, yet he was only supposed to be twenty-five, going on twenty-six. What was going on here? Was this beginning of the end? Was the process accelerating? Sometimes, looking at his hands, they would shrivel up in his mind's eye and it would flash before him that he was actually seventy-six, his real age now, and that it would be revealed to the world at any moment that he was an old man, a senior citizen, anonymous. It would be a catastrophe for himself and his young family. It didn't help that Hicks was also looking unhealthier, his state clearly deteriorating as so often happened to the disabled who spent their lives restricted to wheelchairs. Sometimes he thought Derek needed the herb more than he did. In fact, he was sure he did. But what difference did it make? He was running out anyway. Where was Gombo?

The day after the Indian Wells tournament he decided to go look for him. Fortunately, Molly was deeply into her research and didn't seem overly concerned he wanted to take a few days for himself in Southern California to relax. Besides, Dan had engineered an excuse, setting up an exclusive interview with the famous coach now broadcaster Paul Annacone at the Tennis Channel studios in Santa Monica. The day after the tournament, he rented an anonymous-looking Nissan and drove back into LA where he had reserved a room in a motel in Studio City, the kind of place he imagined he was not likely to be recognized. It wasn't so simple. The clerk at check-in - who had the typical LA look of a slightly long in the tooth out of work actor - knew who he was immediately. Worse, it turned out the man gave tennis lessons in his spare time and insisted on helping Dan to his room, congratulating him endlessly on the tournament victory while commenting on every one of his matches. He evidently had seen them all.

Dan waited for the man to leave and then gave it an extra half hour before he got into the Nissan and headed toward Reseda. It was a hot day and the homeless were congregating beneath the freeway underpasses. There were a lot of them, more than he had ever seen before, sprawled out on blankets and peeking out from the tents - some quite colorful, recent models from REI and North Face - that lined the sidewalks in places almost as far as the eye could see. Some were having sex, or some version of it, scarcely disguised by the tent flaps. Others were defecating in alleys or peeing between parked cars. More than a few seemed to be transgendered, garishly made up, their necks swathed in purple or pink scarves although the temperature was already well up in the eighties in March. Garbage was strewn everywhere. It was the way he would have imagined Calcutta, people in the brightest colors but living in abject poverty. But maybe that was unfair to Calcutta. He had never been there. This was sadder because it wasn't the Third World. This was America. Los Angeles, the city of his dreams when he was young, the golden destination enshrined in song by the Mommas and the Papas, had gone to shit.

The mini-mall, however, seemed much as it had been when he drove up. The nail salon, though still boarded up, hadn't moved and the Institute of Hypnotherapy remained in place as if it would reopen at some point for another generation of gullible divorcees looking for an easy road to a therapist's license.

Gelber parked and made his way to the red door with the sign he remembered well - "Ayurvedic Cures - Open 7 Days" - and knocked. No one responded. Listening closely, he could hear muffled sounds within. Someone was there. He knocked again. And a third time, calling out, "Gombo, it's me. Gelber! Or... Anyway, are you there? Gombo... Gombo..." He pounded again, when he heard shuffling and the door swung open. A skanky woman in a tank top that was half on was standing there. She was missing teeth, had bags under her eyes and needle marks up both sides of her arms.

"Mookie, a cop!" she screamed out.

"A cop? No way. I'm ... "

Suddenly there was a flash of a knife as someone rushed at him, a huge biker type with a pony tail and arms covered with tattoos over every inch of skin. He looked like a linebacker gone to seed. Instinctively, Dan hunkered down, bending over to protect himself. A body was on top of him, slashing away. For a moment he panicked, flashing backwards and thinking he was still a man in his seventies and this was the end. His back would be broken and a knife plunged in his ribs. But then he remembered he was a world class athlete in his twenties who could deadlift 450 pounds and sprung upwards. The man went flying, a knife skittering across the floor. But the man didn't quit. He grabbed a dirty syringe from several lying there and came at Gelber again. Oh, great - heroin, fentanyl, HIV, hep, God-knows-what, Bubonic plague.

Dan took a step backwards and, using one of the drop kicks he drilled many times in practice, the ones his trainer said built the glutes better than squats in half the time while giving him the flexibility to hit unreturnable running overheads from behind the service line, slammed the man hard in the jaw with the heel of his foot. He heard a loud crack as the man flew over backwards landing on his skull. Time stopped still. Blood trickled from the man's nose and mouth upwards towards his nose ring.

"You killed him! You killed Mookie!" yelled the woman, starting to sob. "Fuckin' cop killed Mookie!"

Several other junkies emerged out of the darkness. "Call the fuckin' police!" someone shouted, incongruously. Dan started to back up, glancing down at Mookie. Was he dead? He thought he could see the man turn his head but maybe he was imagining or hoping. He was bending for a closer look when he caught a glimpse of another man waving a steel pipe. No, it was a shotgun. Dan bolted and ran as shot riddled the walls. Out the door, he raced passed his rental - no time to get in - and down an alley as fast as his well-trained legs could carry him. He ran and ran. It was like going for a drop shot that never quite took that second bounce and hung there in suspended animation. He rounded a corner and soon he was out on Reseda Boulevard in front of a Denny's. Without thinking, he ducked inside and sat down at the counter, trying to decide what to do, thinking he was hearing the crackling sound again, someone shouting "Get out!" when he felt a buzz in his pocket. He pulled out his cellphone, fearing, somehow, it was the police already and he was nailed. Was it their siren he was hearing all along?

It was Molly. He might as well answer.

"Hello."

"Hi, daddy," It wasn't Molly. It was Lucas, using his mother's phone. And he sounded excited. "You're so great!"

"No, I'm not."

"Yes, you are. You are! Tell him, mommy."

Dan could hear some whispering as Molly took the phone. "Hi, sweetheart. They want you?"

"What? Who?"

"Are you okay?"

"Yeah… no… I'm fine."

"Yes or no?"

"I'm fine. I said - I'm fine." He thought for a second to confide in her but that would have opened the proverbial can of worms something fierce. How to explain he was out in Reseda in the first place? What was he doing there? And why was he sticking his head in some drug addict's crash pad? I was looking for Gombo wouldn't work. To say the least. That would initiate a discussion that could only lead to ruin. But what else could he say? Was there another excuse? He didn't even know if he'd killed Mookie. Maybe he should be praying for him.

"Well you should be fine because they picked you." By this point Dan realized something that was supposed to be very good had happened. "We're going to Monte Carlo. You won the Laureus!"

In normal circumstances this would have been thrilling and he tried to tell himself that it was anyway. The Laureus World Sports Award for Sportsman of the Year was considered to be the Oscar of sports or at least it was trying to be. The initial winner, when it started back in 2000, had been Tiger Woods who was honored the first two years in a row. He was followed by Michael Schumacher - the Formula One driver -, Lance Armstrong, Federer - four times-, Usain Bolt - the world's fastest man won three times -, Nadal, Djokovic - four times -, Sebastian Vettel - another Formula One driver - and now Jay Reynolds. They seemed to favor tennis players and race car drivers.

"Are you there?" That was Molly. "My father's so happy he thinks he's died and gone to Heaven. It's the first time he's felt good in months. He was trying to reach you. Was your cellphone off?"

"Yeah…. Battery went dead." Couldn't he think of a better excuse the that?

"Where are you?"

"Los Angeles. You know that. Headed for the Tennis Channel studio for my interview." Dan felt as if he were going to be sick.

"Are you excited?"

"Yes. Of course."

"You don't sound it."

"Well, I am. How could I not be? This is great." Maybe he could get away with it, he thought. It was self-defense after all. Maybe he could just pretend it never happened. "I'll be home tomorrow. I love you."

"I do too. So does Lucas."

Later, Dan remembered how Gombo had asked him, high in the Himalayas, you want to be writer again, you want to win Oscar this time, even Nobel Prize? Dan had demurred. Not that. He didn't want to go through the pain of writing again, the endless hours hitting the delete button on his computer. So he had said, no, he wanted something different this second life, he wanted to come back as a tennis player. Now he had won the Oscar of sports. Why wasn't he happy? It was almost as if he had been cursed.

XIII
PLAYING FOR TIME

For the last two years, every morning he wasn't on the road he went out to exercise in his gym, the one he had built in the back yard of the North San Diego County estate next to the three tennis courts and the indoor court that had just finished construction and was meant to replicate the steamy, almost intolerable, conditions of the US Open in the remodeled Arthur Ashe Stadium. There was also now a guest house where a practice partner, often the best of the college crop or an up and comer from somewhere in the top 100, someone who could give him at least the semblance of a fight, could come and stay. The whole complex had been the subject of a recent spread in Town & Country where it was compared to Pete Sampras' California estate, but that only had one tennis court.

But it was the gym that held Dan's attention every morning and was the first place he went, usually as early as he could, before his trainer arrived, even before the maintenance people came to wipe down the state of the art equipment that exercised every muscle group utilized in tennis, which was virtually all of them. These crack of dawn visits had become obsessive, but it wasn't just to get an early start on his exercise program. He wanted to make sure they were still there, that no one had found them, those few of Gombo's pills that were left. They were hidden in a secret container at the bottom of a steel chest on top of which was a set of Russian kettle bells whose meticulous arrangement said please do not touch. There were only six of the pills at this point and a couple of spoonfuls of the tea in a Ziploc bag. It reminded Dan of his clandestine marijuana stash back when he was twenty-three in his previous life. All in all, it was not much, and he guarded what was left with his life, knowing that he might not ever get more.

He had followed this pattern ever since returning from Monte Carlo. He had stood there at the Laureus award ceremony forcing himself to smile graciously while feeling agonized inside. Molly noticed. "What's wrong? Are you sick, sweetheart?" she whispered to him. "Maybe", he said, then thought better of it. "No, I'm fine. I'm just, you know..." concerned that he could have killed someone, he might have added. Or concerned that WADA would soon unmask him and the whole world would judge him a fraud. Or concerned that he would run out of pills, get old and look his age with Molly still in her twenties. How could he justify that? How could he explain what he had done to her? He thought of those Woody Allen movies where the middle aged - or was it late middle-aged - hero was obsessed with teenage girls, romancing them as if it were the most natural thing in the world, how repellent that had become in recent years. But that wasn't him. After all, Molly was an adult. She was even older than he was by a couple of years - or at least she thought she was.

Adding to his bleak mood was an email Dan received the night before the Laureus ceremony only minutes after checking into his hotel. It was from his son Zack. "Hi Jay," it went. "Sorry to disturb you in your moment of glory but you'll excuse me if I'm a bit angry with you. I have just lost my job with Nike. Their reason was that I never delivered the endorsement contract with you I had promised. I guess that was my bad for bragging to them that I could do it, but I thought we had a mind meld. Anyway, had to get this off my chest. Best of luck in your future endeavors, though I don't think you'll need it. Zack Gelber."

Feeling as if he were punched in the proverbial stomach, Dan scrolled the numbers on his cell phone and dialed.

"Hello, Jay," Zack jumped in, obviously having read the display on the other end. "You didn't have to call. I was just —"

"I'm sorry about what happened. I wish it could've been otherwise. I didn't—"

"No matter.... You signed with Uniqlo. Must've been a good deal, considering what they gave Federer."

"It was okay."

"We would have matched it and more. I had it all teed up." Zack's tone was dark. "Now I'm…"

"You're not having problems, are you? Didn't, um, your father leave you something in his will?"

"Yeah, he left me a little more than half a million. I know it sounds greedy but I was hoping it could have been a bit more. He was a successful writer - for a while anyway. But it is what it is."

"Maybe he had to take some of it with him."

"Like an Ancient Egyptian?"

He was joking but it stung inadvertently. Dan Gelber remembered bringing Zack to the Tutankhamen exhibition when he was little boy, how they had marveled at all the useless items the Egyptians brought with them into the afterlife.

Dan cleared his throat. "At least you've got some back up while you look for a new job."

"Unfortunately, not much. I might've told you. My youngest son has an autism spectrum disorder."

"The one named Peter."

"Yeah. It gets expensive, even with insurance. I think we're going to have to move out of the New York area. Go someplace cheaper like Omaha or Detroit. It's just the autism is…"

"This is my fault. I didn't sign for reasons I can't tell you, but…. I have plenty of money. I'll send you something."

"No, no, please. I didn't contact you for a handout."

"I'm serious."

"I'm practically old enough to be your father," he said. How cock-eyed was that? "I couldn't take it. I'd be embarrassed."

"What if I sent it anyway?"

"No, please, no. I… just no." He sounded firm. "Thank you, Jay. I really appreciate your concern. But I'm a grown man and I can't take your money. I'm just short. I'm not a charity case. Good luck in the Laver."

He hung up. Dan stood there, his head ringing. What should he do? Should he send money anyway and insult his own son. These were problems Goethe never wrote about in Faust, Dan Gelber thought, trying to console himself with a little black comedy as once more he did a double check on his stash of Himalayan herbs beneath the kettle balls in his gym. Everything was intact. He had learned to husband them, especially so since, little more than a week after the Laureus, he had been selected to play in what would be for him the most fateful of all tennis competitions, the newly-minted Laver Cup. That event was intended to supersede, indeed already was superseding, the Davis Cup, which had become slightly moribund and often ignored by the best players. This would be, as its website trumpeted, "tennis as you've never seen it before," meaning it would be a convocation of the celebrities of the sport, amped up. Dan, or rather Jay, was part of Team World competing against Team Europe. The Euros were favored because that team consisted of no less that Novak Djokovic, Raphael Nadal and Roger Federer with some backups like Marin Cilic. Team World was mostly Dan, that is Jay Reynolds, along with Juan-Martin Del Potro and some others, some Canadians that had never made it past the semis of a slam, that, if one were being honest, good as they were, were practically useless against the mighty Europeans. Dan would have to win every singles match - he was allowed a maximum of two over the three days - plus his doubles to even make a dent. The event, already staged twice, once in Prague and once in Chicago, had both times been a romp for Europe. The new one would be in Geneva, Federer territory, but the press were already proclaiming Dan the Great American Hope. He had already won at the slams. If someone could bring back the tattered tennis reputation of the United States, Jay Reynolds could.

John McEnroe himself from the heroic era of US tennis was going to be the coach of the World Team, but Hicks—although looking more and more infirm; he wouldn't miss this for, well, the world—would come along to coach Dan personally. Bjorn Borg would coach Europe, as he had done successfully twice before. In truth, the World Team had a chance for the first time because of Dan. Federer, as great as he was, was finally on his last legs and Nadal, due to the constant physicality of his play, had turned his knees into painful pin cushions often making him unable to compete. Only Djokovic - who would be playing two singles matches and doubles just as Dan would - of the once vaunted Big Three remained as a significant adversary who might stop him. And that would only happen if Dan's paltry stash did not hold out or had weakened in some way as medicines do when they drift past their expiration date. How much had Gombo's herbs deteriorated, Dan wondered? Did they have a half-life like Ambien or Xanax? No, they were nature's gift, God's bounty growing wild in the Himalayas and Siberia only. They didn't degrade like the man-made constructs of pharmaceutical companies. They would be fine, Dan Gelber tried to reassure himself. He would be able to stave off the Serb.

XIV
GENEVA

The third contesting of the global Laver Cup was to be played in the Palexpo, a recently remodeled convention center near Geneva's international airport. Like the rest of the city, it was clean, neat and boring, also rich. Dan had been to Switzerland several times in his previous life and it always reminded him of Orson Welles' famous speech from The Third Man - "In Switzerland they had brotherly love - they had 500 years of democracy and peace, and what did that produce? The cuckoo clock." That wasn't entirely fair, Dan Gelber knew. Besides the cuckoo, they manufactured more watches of various sorts from luxury to economy than anyone could imagine and then there was CERN, the nuclear research facility with the biggest particle physics lab in the world, on the cutting edge of virtually everything. And when it came to tennis, Federer and Stan Wawrinka alone had long made them the most successful country on the planet on a per capita basis.

So Dan expected a strongly-biased Swiss, or at least pro-Euro, crowd for the event and was astonished to find, warming up for the first match, that the venue, at least the audience part of it, was festooned with American flags brought by a huge contingent of Yanks shouting "USA! USA!" from the moment Jay Reynolds walked out of the tunnel from the dressing room. Minutes later, as Dan started practicing his serve, someone yelled "Reynolds, wrap 'em up!" channeling the aluminum foil company. The crowd loved it and began a chant of "Reynolds, Reynolds, wrap 'em up!" Soon they were doing the wave. Feet were stomping. People were jumping up and dancing. It was wild. Dan felt as if he were at a soccer match not a tennis competition, though he knew the Davis Cup could be like this, particularly in foreign countries. But these were Americans - in Switzerland! Where did they all come from? The lines at the Eiffel Tower must have dwindled to nothing. The Palexpo grandstands were a sea of red, white and blue. It was as if every American tourist from Dublin to Athens had suddenly decided to descend on Geneva for the Laver Cup. The event might as well have been in New York. But New Yorkers were too blasé. It was clear these people had come to see him - the great American hope.

Given his present concerns, Dan was at best ambivalent about this adulation. Could he live up to it? Did he still have the right stuff, even with his dwindling herb supply? Or would disaster strike and he be carted off during the middle of the tie? "Reynolds, Reynolds, wrap 'em up!" The shouting was reaching a din as the umpire signaled the end of the warm up. Glancing over at his box, he could see Molly enthusiastically waving a flag of her own. Lucas and Olivia, seated on Molly's lap, had them too. Hicks, who had been breathing heavily before the match, raised his hand in a thumb's up. Dan forced a smile in their direction and blew a kiss before he was called to the net by the umpire.

His first match against David Goffin was uneventful. He defeated the Belgian in straight sets, four and three, and was barely challenged. With the Laver Cup's sped up no-add scoring, Goffin had only one break point that Dan whisked away with a sliced backhand at the Belgian's feet. At match point, the crowd started chanting "USA" alternating with "Team World!" so loudly the umpire had to call for silence. Dan finished it off with an ace straight up the T and rushed to the net to shake hands with Goffin. But as he did so, he noted he was feeling unusually tired for such a short match that lasted only an hour and twelve minutes. He seemed on the edge of passing out, as if he had just played one of those five setters with an endless tie breaker that lasted until three in the morning. His head was spinning and his stomach churning. He doubled over after shaking Goffin's hand, gasping for breath and stopping himself from exhaustion.

This continued as he was mobbed by the other members of Team World and his coaches. Politely, and with what little strength he had, he pushed through them to his wife. "I'm not feeling well," he whispered to her. "I'll be right back." Before Molly could reply, he turned and headed as quickly as he could without drawing undue notice for the tunnel. He didn't even look at the fans who were reaching for him, holding out their souvenir tennis balls for an autograph. He normally stopped to sign but proceeded directly through the tunnel to the locker room. He went immediately into a private rest room, locked the door behind him and went to the basin to throw water on his face which felt flushed. When he looked up, he was shocked. Confronting him in the mirror was something her hadn't seen in several years, the visage of - he would guess - a forty-five to fifty-year-old man. He was aging.

Dan Gelber had, of course, feared this for a long time, indeed had known somewhere in his conscious/unconscious from the beginning that such a development was inevitable, but he had repressed it for reasons that were all too obvious. It would have destroyed any pleasure he had in the experience, in his success. Being "The Goat" would have meant nothing. With all that came with it, it would have been no more than a temporary mirage.

"Hey, what's going on, buddy? You okay? You played a helluva match out there. You want the trainer or maybe a doc? You got that doubles tomorrow." Gelber easily recognized the voice of Team World's coach, John McEnroe.

"I'm alright. Just some stomach thing. Think I'll skip the team dinner. See you in the morning."

"Well, you know your body."

"I guess."

Dan waited for McEnroe to leave, then stood there another few minutes before slipping out the door and making a beeline for the player's parking area where he knew his driver would be stationed. "Take me into the city," he said, jumping into the limo and slamming the door. "What about your family?" the driver asked, but Dan simply shook his head and took out his cellphone, punching Molly's number.

"Oh, thank God. Where are you?"

"In our limo… Listen, sweetheart, … I think… I think I've got some kind of fungus or growth on my face."

"You have? Let me look at it. You married a doctor."

"It's not your specialty and I'm already on the way to emergency.… Maybe they can find me a dermatologist. Anyway, it's kind of embarrassing. I really don't want you or the kids to see me this way. It'd freak you out. So get someone to take you all back to the hotel and I'll see you later."

He hung up to avoid getting himself in deeper trouble.

"You want me to take you to hospital, Mr. Reynolds?" said the driver.

"No, no... a, um... costume store." He looked down at his hands. They were wrinkling too. He would need gloves.

It took several hours for Dan Gelber to find what he wanted, what he thought might be the exact right mask to disguise his aging visage. On a certain level, he knew it was ridiculous, but he couldn't think of another solution, at least one that might have a chance of buying him some time, because time was what he thought he needed more than anything.

"Hey, Captain America! That's you, isn't it, daddy?" Luke looked up groggily from his bed in their hotel suite. Dan had hoped he and his sister would be fully asleep when he returned but no such luck.

"Wow," said Molly, gesturing to the mask. "You really must have some awful growth."

"Childhood eczema. I had a horrible case and it seems to have come back. Must be stress. You wouldn't want to see it," said Dan, ducking into the bathroom and shutting the door behind him. "Playing for your country is harder than for yourself," he called out, hoping that would diminish inquiries or at least deflect them.

Running the sink water near maximum to cover whatever sounds or exclamations he would be making, he gingerly removed his mask. The results he saw in the mirror were even more shocking. He was no Dorian Gray with his youth preserved in a painting - that was clear. Since leaving the arena, he seemed to have aged another seven or eight years. He wasn't near his actual true total of seventy-five yet, but, at this rate, it seemed inevitable that he would be - and soon.

Gelber opened the small sack he had brought with him that contained the herbs. There were three pills left and what appeared to be about one tablespoonful of tea. He had no idea what their remaining potency might be. Where was Gombo? Where had he gone? Dan Gelber felt betrayed in his time of need. But how could he have been surprised?

Regarding the Laver Cup, Dan had two more days of play to deal with, each day increasingly more important than the preceding one for the point total of his team. Those were the rules of the three-day cup, designed for escalating tension and drama, weighted really, to the final day when the competition would most often be decided. His victory against Goffin had netted one point. The next days' doubles would be two points and his final singles on Sunday, destined to be against Djokovic again, would be for three points. How could he possibly defeat the Serb under these circumstances? And then there was everything else. He was deep in Sir Walter Scotts' web now. "If first you practice to deceive…" There was no going back. He took a breath and swallowed two of the pills, washing them down with a glass of water.

Not surprisingly, Molly was awake when he walked back into the bedroom. "You're going to keep that thing on?" she said, as he climbed into bed. "Did they give you some medicine for that? Augmentin should take it right out."

He shook his head. "They said it would go away in a few days by itself and to just keep it covered." He peered at her for a moment through the slits in the mask, trying to discern if she believed him. How could she, he thought? Suddenly Dan Gelber was overwhelmed with guilt, a guilt so strong he found himself compelled to say to Molly what had been inside him since they first met, to confess in a way he hadn't since he was in the safety of Dr. Silvera's office. He looked earnestly at Molly. "Suppose there were something about me you didn't know? Would you still love me?"

"It would depend on what it was, I suppose. But I think so. I hope so… What's going on, Jay?" She looked him over slowly. "You're not having an affair, are you? That's not what that masks about it, is it? Because if—"

"No, no. Nothing like that." He rolled over in bed and stared at the ceiling. "Suppose… Suppose, for example, you were married to someone fifty years older than you are. How would you feel about that?"

"Feel about it? What kind of a question is that? It sounds like a fairy tale."

"But suppose it wasn't. Suppose you were married to someone who appeared much younger than he really was?"

"By fifty years? You mean Rip Van Winkle?"

"Suppose there was some way it could happen?"

"What would that be?"

"I don't know. A magic pill or some…. herbal tea brewed by a shaman."

"A shaman, eh? Not a lot of those around here. What about one of those anti-aging creams from Estée Lauder? My friend Linda says they work."

"No, seriously. Answer me." He turned back to her.

"How am I supposed to answer that? Fifty years older? I can't even imagine what that would be like. I'd feel like some child in Afghanistan sold into marriage with a disgusting tribal elder with no teeth. Luckily, I happen to be married to someone two years younger than I am. …. Even if he's so shy he won't let me see his face when he's got a few pimples. That's more like a kid than a seventy-year old... Anyway, you've got a match tomorrow. You should get some sleep."

She switched off the light. Dan Gelber didn't fall asleep for several hours. And after he did finally drift off, he woke up exhausted.

Fortunately for him, his partner was Jack Sock, probably the best doubles player in the world at the moment with a killer net game. More relaxed in doubles than in singles, Sock was also able to use his devastating topspin forehand, which produced virtually as many rotations per minute as Nadal's and had, if anything, more racket-head speed, to great effect against Team Euro's duo of Zverev and Dmitrov. All went pretty well for the first few games - Sock was prowling the net - but by 4-3 the Europeans were getting the picture that Dan's backhand was failing badly and started to pound it. Then he was muffing his once reliable forehand. In minutes they had won the set.

"Ditch the face mask, Captain America," said McEnroe, as Dan came off the court. "You're sweating like a dog under there and blinding yourself."

"Can't. Eczema."

"Think anybody gives a shit about some pimples? Win the fucking game."

Dan nodded and reached into his bag for a drink that he had prepared for himself. It was a mix of Gatorade and Vitamin Water with the last of the pills and herbal tea. It was now or never. He'd deal with tomorrow tomorrow. As he unscrewed the lid, he glanced over at Hicks who was sitting nearby. "You can do it, Jay," he said in a voice that was strained and barely audible. "Take the ball early. Cut down their time. Keep moving in to control the points." Dan was about to snap back at him but restrained himself because of the man's health. It was the same litany he had heard time and again, since he first played tennis, from Hicks and every other coach he had ever had, even as a twelve-year old Dan Gelber taking lessons in a public park. But try as he might, he could never actually do it, at least not effectively, until he ran into Gombo and his concoctions. Only then did he have the necessary energy and aggression. Only then did he succeed on a level to which he aspired, whether on the court or anywhere else. Some were meant for greatness, others, as Milton noted, only stood and waited.

What cheap irony, Dan thought - why did he think of that - as he drank almost all the contents of the bottle, saving the last, hardly much more than a swallow but something, for the next day's match before walking back on the court for the second set: They also serve who only stand and wait. Serve what? Serve where? To the back hand? Down the middle? What did that have to do with serving God, so obviously Milton's meaning in his sonnet? He asked himself that question as he whistled one by Dimitrov. Well, maybe it did serve God in some way. Aesthetic? It kept one in the moment - any Zen master and sports coach would approve. At least he was playing better. The herbs were kicking in. Perhaps these last pills actually still had some potency. He was feeling himself again, that is his new self, not his old self. If only he could get more of those herbs, he could go forever this way, or at least until an actuarially predicted 83, a number that was sufficiently distant in his new life, if looming all too close in his old.

He and Sock were able to turn the match around, winning the second set 6-4 and going into the ten-point tie breaker the Laver Cup's organizers had chosen, in lieu of a long and possibly tedious third set, to rapidly advance the action for today's impatient audiences. Before he knew it, Sock-Reynolds were out front 4-1. Then it was 7-2. Soon Dan was serving for the match, hitting out wide to Dimitrov's backhand with a little extra kick to stretch the Bulgarian out even further. Sock put away the feeble return. Team World mobbed them. They were ahead of Team Europe for the first time. In fact, they were ahead of Team Europe the first time in the three years of the competition.

The jubilation continued as the team - world-class athletes locked together arm-in-arm like schoolboys, jumping up and down on imaginary pogo sticks - headed down the corridor to the locker room. But just as Dan was about to enter, he was confronted by Dr. Withers. She was standing there with a tall, elderly gentlemen with long silvery hair who looked Indian or Pakistani.

"Good afternoon, Mr. Reynolds. Congratulations on another victory. Quite an amazing recovery you made after that first set," said Withers.

"Gatorade will do it every time."

She nodded noncommittally and gestured to her companion. "Allow me to introduce Professor Bannerjee, of the Kolkata College of Herbal and Ayurvedic Medicine."

"Very excited to meet you, Mr. Reynolds. I have so wanted introduction for some time. We have much to discuss between us…. By the way, I was tennis player too. In my youth, number four in West Bengal."

"Nice to meet you too... But if you'll excuse me, I think I need a shower." Dan started for the locker room

"Yes, yes. Take shower. We wait."

"Not necessary. It may take me a while. I'm gonna need a long shower. Tough match, you know. I really stink."

"We will wait," said Withers calmly. No doubt she meant it.

Moments later, Dan entered a private shower room, locking the door behind him. He was carrying his tennis bag with him, something he wouldn't normally do, but the "Gatorade" bottle was in one of the pouches and he didn't want it out of his site. He also had a fresh set of clothes with him and hanged them on the hook. Then he took off his sneakers and his sweaty tennis togs, letting them drop to the floor beneath the changing bench next to a waiting laundry bag. Lastly, he removed the mask and put that on the bench away from the shower so it wouldn't get wet. He didn't bother to glance at the mirror hanging over the basin. He didn't want to look. There was no telling how he appeared now. The old man and the sea? Methuselah? Who knew? Just as he was about turn on the shower, the voice of John McEnroe called through the door. "Hey, Captain America, I was wrong for once. Keep wearing that thing-um tomorrow. Very patriotic!"

"Sure," Dan said, turning on the shower and stepping under it immediately, before it was barely warm. "USA! USA!" he intoned. He hoped the water pouring onto his head would spring some idea of what he should do, just as the steady flow of H2O had often broken fits of writer's block in the old days. But there was no such luck this time. His brain was still clouded, actually on the edge of panic. It was fight or flight and he couldn't see what fight would do. Nevertheless, he counseled himself, he should do his best to calm down, play along for a bit. After all, it had been well more than a year since his lengthy sojourn at Bellevue Medical Center and he had heard nothing. He had assumed that was good news. In fact, he had been listed as medically clear on a private WADA website he had perused late one night, using a password given him by the Association of Tennis Professionals. But the presence of Professor Bannerjee was more than a little disturbing. Herbal and Ayurvedic Medicine - they had clearly found something. But how?

He found out later while meeting with Withers and Bannerjee in the now empty arena. They were seated in what was formerly his supporter's box. Dan had texted Molly to have their driver take her back to the hotel. He had to stay late. He didn't bother to explain why because he couldn't think of an excuse that wouldn't be transparently suspicious. Perhaps he could later, but he suspected he was already too far gone in Walter Scott's web of deception to devise anything remotely plausible.

"We found trace of herb I in no circumstance, previous in nature or laboratory, have seen evidence," the professor was saying in Anglo-Indian sentence construction so convoluted Dan could barely make sense of it, but the gist was inescapable. "Resembles rhodiola but not exactly that. Maybe second cousin once removed."

"What's rhodiora?" Dan deliberately mispronounced it, although he knew perfectly well what it was. Two minutes into the conversation and he was already deceiving again.

"Herb from Himalaya and Siberia promotes manifestation of what your civilization call fountain of youth, but Western doctors claim no scientific study in support. I would beg to disagree, but I am no more than humble professor from far away West Bengal."

"That depends on where you start..." Where had he found the energy to make such a prolix joke?

"Oh, yes. Very funny. All is relative. Not so far from East Bengal, as you say."

"How is it you came to discover whatever this mysterious herb is exists in my system? Where'd that come from?"

"From your Bellevue workup," Withers interjected.

"I don't understand. I saw the record months ago. No drugs indicated. The report was clean."

"We did too until we got an alert we could not ignore."

"About what?"

"Your behavior. It made us go back and look again at your tests. One of the doctors saw the similarity to rhodiola."

"That is why they contact me," said Bannerjee. "For expert opinion."

"Who sent this alert?" Dan was starting to sweat. It wouldn't have been a good time for a polygraph.

"I'm sorry. That's a confidence from a colleague I am not at liberty to disclose."

"Well, that's terrific. How am I supposed to react? Am I banned from the sport now?"

"Not necessarily.... Why're you still wearing that mask, if you don't mind my asking?" Withers was squinting at him. "The match is over."

"Because I have eczema. Would you like to be grossed out? … Also, I admit it—it embarrasses me," he added, feigning contrition. "But I'll take it off, if you wish."

"That's not necessary, Mr. Reynolds. Professor Bannerjee would like to ask you a few questions. We have to ascertain if this substance, rare as it may be, should be proscribed. It could relate to every sport, not just tennis. We have an Olympic games coming up."

"Not until you tell me where you got this alert."

"Unfortunately, as I indicated, that is confidential information. But this person, who is in the helping professions, said you were behaving very strangely."

"The helping professions? You don't mean a psychiatrist, by any chance?" Dan Gelber had a flash of insight that wasn't much of a flash. It could have been no one else but Dr. Emanuel Silvera. The doctor was the only one he had ever spoken to about the herbs. What a mistake that apparently was—his own ambivalence toward psychotherapy coming back to haunt him. "If that is so," Dan continued, "whatever I told him was supposed to be confidential. It's against the law to—"

"I'm sorry. We are not at liberty to disclose—"

"And we were only exploring my fantasies, as people do in therapy…. Nothing about it was real. I can't imagine why he would have thought so." But as he said that Dan Gelber realized that Silvera would not have to think what Gelber was telling him was literally true to be concerned. The essence of it was there. Moreover, the doctor was himself a tennis player and, considering the extraordinarily rapid rise of Jay Reynolds, would likely be more suspicious of doping, whatever the source, Eastern or Western, than the average shrink. How naive of Dan to have chosen him. It was proving to be a fatal error.

"All we can say is that the professional who contacted us was concerned with your well-being," said Withers, her head tilted slightly downward. Dan realized then she and Bannerjee as well were staring directly at the tennis bag Gelber was clutching unconsciously and almost religiously to his chest as if it were his most precious possession. And indeed, it was. He tried to relax his fingers, but somehow they wouldn't move. Was this the end of the game? Was he finally caught?

"You have great affection for bag, Mr. Reynolds," Bannerjee spoke with great politeness. "I see is special one with badges for your magnificent grand slam victories—Roland Garros, Wimbledon and so forth, all lined up in order of accomplishment. I have seen this before with other players of your most extraordinary standing, also sometimes on shoes. Perhaps inside is something even more valuable you would share with us for benefit of science."

"I don't know what you're talking about. My underwear?"

But before he could get a response, Dan Gelber was again distracted, and seemingly out of nowhere, by the crackling sound, someone yelling "Get out! Get out!" Louder and louder. He couldn't get away from it. Where was it coming from? Who was doing this? Was he going mad?

He looked around for the source when Bannerjee jumped forward and snatched his tennis bag from his hand, ripping open the zipper and extracting the Gatorade bottle.

"What're you doing with that?" Dan reached for the bottle, but Bannerjee stepped back.

"Is Gatorade? I saw you drinking between sets. And then your game improves as if by magic. I am tennis player and I know. In first set I could beat you."

"That's total nonsense. I was out of energy. Had some Gatorade like everybody else. It's normal."

"No, no… not normal." He opened the Gatorade bottle and sniffed it. "Smells like dirt from mountain after monsoon, not sweet at all. More like sour herbal cough medicine. Look…"

He passed the bottle over to Withers who started to smell it herself when Dan lunged for it and snatched it back. He spun around quickly, making a mad dash for a nearby bathroom with Withers and Bannerjee in pursuit.

"Give it back, Mr. Reynolds," said Withers, as they caught up with him. "Otherwise you will be banned immediately." She and Bannerjee started advancing on him, backing him against a row of urinals. "The authorities know we are here and are expecting a report."

"I'm telling you, you're wrong," Dan replied. "This is Gatorade. It just has a peculiar flavor tailored to my weird taste." Withers and Bannerjee stopped in front of him and stared. They weren't buying it. He hadn't expected they would. He held out the bottle for them anyway. "See?" Before they could respond. He spun around again, turned over the bottle and rapidly poured the remaining contents – there was less than a quarter of the original amount anyway – directly into the nearest urinal and flushed it down, the last of whatever the compound was that had made his new life. At this point, he had no choice. He really was cornered and it only would have been a matter of days in any case. The end was nigh. Game, set, match, tournament and Dan was the loser. At least this way the evidence would be almost impossible to obtain and the public spectacle diminished. He hoped so anyway. "Sorry, folks," he said to the nonplussed Withers and Bannerjee and bolted for the door.

Dan kept running until he was out of sight, but then slowed deliberately and walked the remaining three kilometers back to the hotel, hoping to collect his thoughts. He had no luck. Dan Gelber's mind was a blank, a first for him in many ways. It was the most depressing walk of his life by any measure, as if he were marching to his own funeral, that is the funeral of his second life.

Molly was waiting up when he returned, sitting on the edge of the bed, holding a glass of whiskey she had poured from the supply in the minibar. Two small Scotch bottles, already empty, were on the end table. Dan took a seat opposite her and they sat there without speaking for what seemed like an hour but was probably more like four minutes.

"What's going on, Jay?" she finally said. "What's all this about?"

Dan said nothing for another minute or so, then slowly, reluctantly, pulled off his mask. Molly gasped.

"My name is Dan Gelber," he began.

Minutes later he had told her a short version of his story - how he, a man in his seventies, had collapsed in the first games of a seniors' tennis tournament and was rushed to the hospital where he had a disastrous back operation, although he was warned against it by a Nepali woman. That woman had advised him to see her uncle in the valley who turned out be to a shaman from the Himalayas that gave him pills that made him young again. He could become Jay Reynolds, international tennis star.

"That's insane," said Molly. "I never heard anything so crazy. It's scientifically impossible." She shook her head back and forth a half dozen times. Dan Gelber watched, a knifing pain going directly into the pit of his stomach. "It's... it's..." Molly continued "Where am I living? Am I on planet Earth? Am I dreaming? I hope I'm dreaming. I have to be dreaming. This is the most..."

She broke down in tears.

"You're not dreaming. It's me. It's just me. I—"

"Just you? What the fuck are you talking about? We have children. How could you do this?"

"We all want to live forever. You know that song. From 'Fame'."

"Another reference to something I never heard of. Now I understand... I think... anyway." The last word was lost in tears.

He had hated himself the moment he had said that. What a dreadful thing to say - or think. And actually the lyrics went "I'm gonna live forever/ Baby, remember my name." But it was Jay Reynolds who was going to live forever, whose name would be remembered, at least in some sports record books even if he quit and never played again, not him, not Dan Gelber. It was all a waste. And nobody lives forever anyway. It was the grandest of illusions only a child would believe. "My name is Ozymandias, King of Kings." Dan had read the Shelley poem in the ninth grade. "Look on my Works, ye Mighty, and despair! Nothing beside remains."

Molly suddenly stopped crying. She sat up straight. "You are the most selfish person I have ever met, if indeed you are an actual human being."

"I am human, unfortunately. In some ways I wish I weren't."

"I hate you."

"You should."

"I hate you... I really hate you." She repeated, then took a long breath, as if she were short of air, and exhaled. "But I also love you. I'm trapped."

"You don't love me. You love Jay Reynolds."

"What am I going to do for the rest of my life? Can't you do something? Take more of those pills or something? ...Go back to being Jay Reynolds, whoever he is."

"There aren't any. Gombo only gave me a limited supply and now he's gone. They're some kind of rare herb. I don't think I could ever find them again."

"A rare herb. How exotic. This Gombo stuff sounds like a fairy tale. No one could possibly believe it. I don't know who you are. For all I know you could be some athlete on a megadose of IV testosterone or some new steroid from Russia one of Putin's scientists invented to turn his Olympic team into super freaks." She held her head in her hands, hyperventilating. "Oh, God, why did you do this to me? And my father? How am I going to tell him? He said I should never marry you and he knew. And then you wanted to start that foundation so he could walk. What was that about? Another charade? ... You know he's gotten worse, don't you? He was hiding it from you during the tournament so you wouldn't be distracted. How pathetic. How sad. But he's having trouble breathing now because of trouble in his respiratory system. It's probably irreversible. Our own department gives him about a year to live. He only came to Geneva because of you." She looked Dan straight in the eye and shook her head slowly. "You know you're right. I don't love you. How could I? What was I thinking? You're just an ugly, bitter old man." She stood up. "Get out. Just get out. I don't ever want to see you again!"

At that point, Olivia wandered into the room. "Mommy, there's a ghost."

XV

ON THE ROAD

Dan Gelber slept in his clothes at an airport hotel that night. He had left without packing and had no pajamas. In any case, they wouldn't have fit him, because he was shrinking, heading back to his original five foot seven—or was it five-six—from six-two and a half. It wasn't just his skin that was aging. It was his entire corpus. Also, his energy had decreased. It was past midnight and he was exhausted by the time he checked into the hotel. Nevertheless, he couldn't sleep. He lay there filled with regret—how could he possibly fix things—hoping no one would notice when he didn't show up for the pre-match workout the next morning. But of course, they would. Within minutes they would call his cellphone, but he had already gotten rid of it, tossing it in a dumpster on the way to the hotel, knowing they could track the damn things even when they were off. He would buy a disposable one later. In the morning he was supposed to play Djokovic, the real best player in the world, not that poseur Jay Reynolds who had succeeded to number one via a magic potion from God-knows-where. What if he actually showed up in his present state, with or without the Captain America mask? What a strange match that would have been, the seventy-something Dan Gelber versus Novak Djokovic. Would he even have won one point? Only if the Serb had double-faulted, always a possibility in a two-set match. But what would the fans have thought of this bizarre one-sided spectacle? They would certainly have a right to be angry with a ticket price starting at 250 euros. The whole idea of such a match was absurd.

He imagined the expression on McEnroe's face when he walked out onto the court as the aging Dan and smiled for a fleeting second at the thought before retreating into his slough of despond and staying there. Tennis was the furthest thing from his mind. He could think of nothing but Molly and his children, all of them, from both lives.

He took the first jitney to the airport that morning. He had booked himself on a seven a. m. Swissair flight to Los Angeles, wondering all the time if he would be able to pass through security as an older man when his passport had him in his twenties. Thankfully, because he was always on the road in the endless eleven-month a year tennis season, he had enrolled in the biometric CLEAR system quite some time ago. It identified you via a code generated from your fingerprints and irises. Those, most likely, would remain relatively the same over decades. And Jay Reynolds, although not quite John Smith, was a common enough name. In fact, the official at the douane joked about it as Dan stood in front of the inspection device that was scanning his pupils. "Are you the great tennis player?" he said with a laugh. "Absolutely," said Dan. "I think I'm missing my match." "Yes, today against Djokovic. No wonder you are leaving." "I dunno. I think I woulda had a shot, don't you?" "*Bien sur*," said the guy with the requisite ironic tone that signaled he was in on the game. Dan winked at the official as the machine buzzed him through. A half hour later he was on the plane, sitting in business, not his usual first, in order to be less conspicuous, although at this point he could not have been more anonymous, an aging businessman on yet one more international flight. Slumped in his seat, he started to feel a nagging pain in his lower back. Was that returning too? Maybe he would need a second operation. Not that he cared. Was there a way to make things right? That was all that mattered at this point. He was skeptical to say the least but wanted to try. He ordered a Scotch with his breakfast and fell into merciful sleep somewhere over the pole, awakening as the plane was in the glide path to LAX.

It was only noon when he arrived and Dan took an Uber - renting a car would have meant showing ID - to his destination, Cedars Sinai Medical Center.

"I'm a patient of Dr. Chung's," he told the reception desk. "Can you tell me where he is?"

"Your name?"

"Gelber... Dan."

"Do you have an appointment?" she frowned, glancing down at her monitor. "Dr. Chung's in surgery this morning."

"I understand," said Gelber, adding as innocently as possible. "Where's that?"

The receptionist gestured to a double door with a sign reading 'Authorized Personnel Only.' "You'll have to make an appointment," she said.

"Of course." Dan nodded and retreated in the opposite direction as the receptionist watched, feeling a twinge in his back again. He hoped it was just the marble floors, but suspected it wasn't. "Perhaps you can let him know I stopped by." He ducked around a corner and stepped into the gift shop.

A few minutes later he stepped out again. The receptionist had been replaced by another woman who was speaking to a maintenance worker. Dan, bent over almost exaggeratedly, walked briskly passed them through the double door. There was an advantage to being an older man - you moved through the world less noticed, similar to the way older women were always complaining about. The sexes were more equal after all.

He walked further down the corridor to a nurse's station and inquired after Dr. Chung. The nurse pointed to an operating room. The red light was lit. He didn't dare enter. How long would he have to wait? He was about to ask the nurse when he spotted the actual person he had come to see. It wasn't Dr. Chung. It was the Indian cleaning woman - really Nepali, he had long realized - who had been in his original operating room. What luck! Maybe there was a God after all, he thought as he felt a sharp pain coursing through his vertebrae just as he had when he collapsed on that tennis court. Clutching a pail and mop, she was heading into what looked like a maintenance room.

Dan loped after her and entered the room as the woman turned toward him, astonished. "Please don't worry," he said before she could scream. "I come in peace.... Do you recognize me?" She stared at him. "You gave me some advice before I was operated on. Remember?" The woman continued to look, unsure. "My back was out, and you said I should see your uncle or cousin in the Valley... I can't remember... Nawang Gombo."

"Nawang Gombo," she repeated. "Yes, I remember. How is back?"

"Not good at the moment. It was better." He paused for affect. "You were right. Gombo helped.... Now..." He shrugged and pressed his palm to his lower back. It was tender. "... I think I need further treatment. And he is the only one I can trust."

"Yes, trust, of course. You trust Uncle Nawang. Why not? So go see."

"Go see where?"

"Where you see in first place." The woman turned away, placing her bucket and mop in the corner while facing away from Gelber as if to dismiss him.

"I wish I could, but he's gone. His clinic is closed now. It's filled with junkies." One of whom he might have killed, he could have added. But it seemed more than extraneous at the moment.

The woman looked at him. "Please, mister, do not make joke with me. Uncle Nawang never let drug addict near clinic for herbal cure. Very bad people."

"Well, I'm telling you something happened in this case. He's not there anymore."

The woman clucked and muttered something in Hindi or Nepali. "You are very wrong, Mister…. Mister…"

"Gelber."

"Yes, Gelber, I remember now. You not listen when I tell you. Have dumb operation. Well, listen this time. I with Uncle Nawang two weeks ago at clinic. We celebrate Diwali five days. Put lights and everything. You know what is Dewali?"

"Yes," he said weakly. It was a big Hindu holiday, he knew that much. What was going on? Had he been seeing things? First the crackling sound and now this.

"You go clinic. You see," she said.

An hour later Dan Gelber was at the mini mall in Reseda again. On his way over there, he had passed some public tennis courts where he used to hit balls with Zack when his son was a kid. Curiously, staring at the court, he remembered one particular time he yelled at young Zack for repeatedly missing some easy over heads, although Dan always had trouble with that shot himself. It was a day a script he had written—one he thought was especially good—was put in "turn around," as they used to euphemistically call it, by the studio. It was far from the first time for Gelber, or for any screenwriter, even the most successful, but still he took it out on his son. He even realized what he was doing while it was happening but didn't have the discipline to stop himself. That was only weeks before he and Cynthia told Zack they were divorcing. The boy ran away in his room and stayed there for what seemed like days. Well, there was nothing he could do about any of that now, Dan Gelber thought. That was then. But he wondered whether Zack hit tennis balls with Peter today and how that went, considering the little boy's problems, his attention difficulties. Gelber realized at that point he didn't know if Peter played tennis at all or ever had. He thought for a moment to call and say hello, try to find out how things were going, but which life did he want - his new one or his old one? He had other responsibilities now, other children—not to mention Hicks and, of course, Molly, the gorgeous, divine Molly. How could he satisfy all at once? And how could he satisfy himself, the onetime international sports celebrity with the world at his feet? Could that ever return? Did he miss it? He had to admit even now that he did, much as he didn't like himself for it, indeed hated himself.

At that moment, and seemingly inevitably, he started to hear the crackling again, accompanied by the usual voices. "Get out! Get out!!" It grew louder, approaching a din. The noise level was incredible, louder than he had ever heard it, louder than when he was backstage at a The Who concert years ago and had to leave, despite having paid scalper prices for the tickets. Now people were screaming. Gelber clutched at his ears, fearing it would make him deaf. But the Uber was pulling up in the mini mall and the noises ended as quickly as they had started.

Dan Gelber, relieved, thanked the driver, got out of the car and surveyed the area. Much was as he had left it. He thought he noticed a few more homeless tents under the freeway underpass across the street, but that was about the extent of the discernible changes. Even Gombo's clinic appeared unaltered with its bright red door and sign reading "Ayurvedic Cures - Open Seven Days."

He walked up to it and knocked, fearing he would have to confront the junkies once again. Would Mookie be there? Was he alive? Or was the cleaning woman correct, that no such thing had happened, that it was still Gombo's clinic and there was no Mookie? But how could that be? Was he dreaming? He knocked again. There was no answer. Emboldened, he cried out, "Gombo, are you there? It's Gelber!" Nothing. Perhaps he should have said Jay Reynolds, but he didn't bother. He tried again. "Gombo!" Still nothing.

He pushed on the door almost reflexively and, to his surprise, it swung open. Dan Gelber stepped gingerly inside, still apprehensive that the clinic had been turned into a crash pad and danger lurked at every corner, but within seconds he saw that was not so. Everything was neat and clean, the way he had first seen it when he met Nawang Gombo, except most of the rooms had been stripped bare, the blow-ups of Everest removed. The shelves were still there but all evidence of herbs, including empty jars, were removed.

Gelber continued into the small back room where Gombo kept his office. He had only been there once. At first it seemed as empty as everywhere else and he was ready to walk back out again, when he noticed a newspaper sitting on an end table. It was the sports section of the *Los Angeles Times* and the banner headline screamed out at him: "WHERE'S JAY?" Beneath was a photo of Djokovic standing alone in the Geneva tennis court in front of a full house of fans with his mouth open and his hands extended in amused bafflement. A smaller photo of Jay was tucked into the corner. Gelber picked up the paper for a closer look, glancing at the article that began "A massive worldwide search is in progress for missing American tennis star Jay Reynolds who disappeared from…"

Dan suddenly stopped reading, his attention caught by an object revealed when he picked up the paper. It was a US passport in a Ziplock bag. Had Gombo left this for him? Dan Gelber was immediately suspicious. He opened the bag, took out the passport and opened it to the front page. The passport was for Dan Gelber with his photo at roughly his current age. Attached to the second page with a staple was an ornate visa for the Russian Republic. Falling out from between the pages was a small travel brochure for Khanty-Mansisysk.

Khanty-Mansisysk?

Khanty-Mansisysk, Siberia, Russian Republic?

What was this? Come, Gombo seemed to be saying, I will give you one last chance. Come to Siberia where the purest of herbs still exist in the great beyond.

But how did he know Gelber had been there before? Had the shaman been watching him his entire life?

XVI

SIBERIA

Dan Gelber had indeed been there before, in his previous life that now seemed to be becoming his present life again. Some years ago his friend Tanya - a former director of the Soviet screenwriters union, now in a similar position under capitalism - had called him with an offer he could not refuse, to be a juror in the first "Spirit of Fire" Film Festival, "to visit Siberia and come back," as he told Ogee what seemed like eons ago. Tanya's accent was laden with the appropriate dark Russian humor that wasn't that far from the Borscht Belt. But it wasn't as dark as Siberia in February, the time of year he had gone to a place indeed called Khanty-Mansiysk in their post-communist nouveau riche oil country. His greatest memory, as he also told Ogee, was arriving massively jet lagged at three in the morning to be serenaded by a chorus of regionally-dressed locals in some form of dirndl singing "M...I... C...K... E....Y." while standing in front of illuminated ice statues of Mickey Mouse and other Disney characters. His second greatest memory was flying in a helicopter looking down at the vast, snowy expanse of the taiga that went as far as the eye could see. How extraordinarily beautiful was the world's largest outdoor prison. Siberia, he was told, constituted almost ten percent of the Earth's land surface. Finding anyone or anything there would be way beyond even locating the proverbial needle in a haystack.

Yet, he would have to do it - track down Gombo in some icy redoubt where roads were cut into snow that went to depths of over a hundred feet.

Beneath, presumably, was the herb the Nepali - and now Dan - was looking for. Was that the secret to eternal life? A frozen piece of vegetation?

But where to start? Careful not to retrace his steps, he asked the Uber driver to leave him at a FedEx store he knew in Glendale. There he rented one of the computers, logging onto his old iCloud account. Everything was still there, including his address book. He took out the disposable cell phone he had recently purchased and dialed. The phone on the other end rang and rang, the party on the other end reluctant to pick up an anonymous international call. Dan typed in a name and tried again. This time it worked.

"Jay Reynolds, missing superstar!... Like David Bowie back from dead."

"Hello, Ogee. I'm no David Bowie."

"You sound terrible. Maybe next Alexander McQueen. Don't hang yourself."

"I'm not so great, to be honest."

"Did you leave your wife? Page Six called. They want to know if we are together finally, ha-ha-ha..."

"You wouldn't want me the way I look now. And, no, I didn't leave my wife. It's... complicated.... Some day maybe I'll explain... I know this sounds stupid, but what do you know about Siberia? "

"I have been there only once. That's the same as you. You told me - remember? You went to a film festival."

"Didn't you say your father had oil wells there?"

"Yes, of course. He has several fields."

"Where are they?"

"Near Khanty-Mansisysk."

"Khanty-Mansisysk?"

"Something wrong with that?"

"I, uh... that's where I was. It's where they had that festival.... This is bizarre."

"Why? Is small-town - became rich from oil in nineties. So they have festival. Bring culture to frozen North. Film stars from Moscow like to go there buy furs. Or maybe get lucky and shaman helps them get part in next movie." She laughed.

"They have shamans?" Why had he asked? He already knew the answer. But he wanted it confirmed.

"Of course - for tourists. With oil boom, real one retreat to country-side. But you know that. You were there. By the way, Novak said very kind things about you when you didn't show for match. Maybe because he had marital problems too."

"That's nice."

"Others not so complimentary. McEnroe…"

"I imagine," he intoned, his voice barely audible.

"Jay, what is matter with you? You sound so - how you say - *deprimido*. Cheer up. You know - times change, people change. That happens." She paused, then became suddenly more playful. "Listen, my gorgeous boychik, I have clever idea for you … Why don't you meet me in Majorca? I make you feel better. I promise. We go to Rafa's tennis camp. You practice, be back to yourself in no time. On way to GOAT again."

"GOAT?"

"Don't be cute. You know everybody say. Greatest of all time. You practically there. Start your comeback in Sydney. We play mixed doubles together. On and off court. Make some gossip."

"I'm not going to be playing in Australia."

"You Americans! So like puritan in funny hat. You're not first man who has problem with marriage. Or first professional athlete run around. Everyone has fun on road. Olympics like orgy. Condom machines run out. Maybe not so nice but so what? Perhaps you marry too young. It's not tragedy unless you make it. First one mistake. Second or maybe third time lucky… You both - you and your Mollika - will be happier in end. You will see. Auntie Ogee guarantee… So, Majorca? I can be there Tuesday, maybe sooner."

"No, Ogee. Sorry… I love my wife. I want her back, but I can't have her."

"Mr. Doom and Gloom."

She clicked off. Dan took a moment to collect himself. It was weird being propositioned at this time, if that's what she was doing. Maybe it was just reflex for her. Nevertheless, here he was with seemingly no choices. Khanty-Mansisysk again. How could that happen? Was something pre-or-dained? Was he in the hands of some shamanistic gods, interconnecting the Himalayas and Siberia? Was Gombo waiting there for him? Had he found some super shaman who held the secret? He was far from believing such paranormal nonsense, even now, but still… He went back to the computer. According to Wikipedia, KM was a town of roughly 80,000 inhabitants. It hadn't seemed that big when he was there - just a small village of pastel cottages that reminded him of Chekov - but how was he to know what it was really like? He hadn't seen a shaman, real or in a tourist costume. He had spent most of his time in the jurors' screening room, watching interminable subtitled movies from Mongolia and Azerbaijan that seemed made before anyone had even thought of hiring a film editor. One of them, he recalled, even did have a shaman in it, dressed in full regalia, howling like a wolf. The makeup job wasn't very good. But he couldn't remember more than that. Because of his jet lag, he was barely awake for most of the films.

More significantly, he learned from his brief web search, Khanty-Mansisysk was part of the Khanty-Mansi Autonomous Okrug, a region of Khanty and Mansi peoples known collectively as Ob Ugric – a shamanistic culture. It was the heartland of shamanism, where it all began. Dan knew he would have to go. He was impelled to do so, ride the endless Aeroflot jet from LAX to Sheremetyevo, as he had before, then take a cab for an hour or more across the city to that other Moscow airport, the one that serviced Asia, Domodedovo, for another three hour flight north-east to Siberia.

On his first trip, he recalled, he was restless, unable to sleep, perhaps apprehensive, as Americans often were, traveling to Russia. But this time, he slept like the proverbial baby, putting himself to sleep by forcing himself to think of the good times with Molly and the children, beach vacations on the Mediterranean and skiing in Switzerland when the snow held up just before clay court season. Sometimes it morphed into vacations with young Zack, not as luxurious but still fun, like when he took his son hiking in Canada after the divorce. They had camped at Lake Louise. Could days like that ever return, Dan Gelber wondered? Would he ever see that kind of peace again? He felt as if he were on a mission to find out, to try to make it happen if it were still in any way possible. But as he lay there, slumped against the fuselage of a 767, it was hard for him to tell whether he was dreaming or day-dreaming or just engaging in the most desperate wish-fulfillment. Whatever the case he felt surprisingly rested when he got off the plane in Khanty-Mansisysk. On this occasion, no chorus of locals was there, nor were there any illuminated ice statues of Disney characters. Also, it was not pitch dark, as it was for most of his February visit. It was summer and still light at 1:34AM. He was in the land of the midnight sun. It was also warm and dry, almost, curiously, like California in autumn. Waiting to be transported to his hotel, he stared out at an endless horizon. What was he doing here? It was madness.

"What brings you to Khanty-Mansisysk, *tovarish*?" the clerk asked Dan as he checked in.

"Looking for a shaman."

"What else?" The man smiled wryly. "When do you want start?"

"It's two in the morning."

"Here no one sleep this time year. In winter we hibernate.

"Like polar bears."

"They do not hibernate. Only black bears…. But if you look shaman, maybe go next door. Someone there might help." He gestured out the window where a bar or night club glowed in the dim light. Dan could hear music and shouting. "I will bring bag to room."

Why not? Dan Gelber nodded his thanks and headed across the street.

XVII
THE GULAG

The Gulag was a karaoke bar announced by a neon sign in several languages. True to its name, it was decorated in neo-Soviet style with Day-Glo portraits of Lenin, Trotsky and Stalin dominating the room. Solzhenitsyn and Sakharov were also represented, but in less prominent black and white images behind the bar, which was shaped like Lenin's tomb with a bobblehead versions of the Politburo lined up across it. Barbed wire hung from the ceiling, adding to the ambience. A man who looked to be East Asian sang "Back in the USSR" in what sounded like some dialect of Chinese.

Dan ordered a vodka from the bartender, a fortyish woman with dark hair and what used to be called a Jewish nose. It wasn't unattractive really but prominent. She reminded him of girls he knew in grammar school in New York. Most of them had nose jobs by the time they were in junior high.

"You are American?" she said.

"How'd you guess?"

"Is not hard. You also probably Russian-Jewish by background. Or maybe Polish. From settlement Pale."

"How do you know that?"

"You look just like my uncle Yitzhak. He lives near Jerusalem. In Ein Kerem. He has angina and everyone say he should retire, but he won't listen. He was always stubborn ox… So, what is name, Mr. American?" She poured him a vodka in a shot glass. "Drink that quickly and then I pour another. Is local style."

"Dan Gelber." He knocked back the vodka.

"Faster next time." She filled the second glass. "Otherwise people here think you weak. Take advantage…. What brings you Siberia in summer? Come to hunt tiger? Is hundreds mile from here."

"I'm looking for a shaman."

"So you be fleeced of money? I thought you Jewish."

"Actually, I'm looking for a friend from Nepal who is looking for a shaman, I think."

"Oh… then you better drink." She gestured to the glass. "Do not worry. Is not strongest vodka." Following instructions, Dan put it down more quickly. "That is Spirytus… 192 proof. This only 178."

Dan's knees started to buckle. "I think that's enough." He put the glass down.

"It should be. How old you. 60?"

"Actually, a bit older."

"You don't look so bad for age. Around here most people fall over 52."

"Hang on a bit longer and I'll be looking my age."

"So why your friend want see shaman?"

"To get young again, I imagine. Like everyone else. Find some Siberian herb to replace his Himalayan herb… He's a shaman too. But I'm not sure he's my friend. Sometimes I think he's the Devil."

"If he is Devil, what he need shaman for? Should be other way around."

"I've been wondering that myself."

"Is five, six hour drive where real shaman live." She studied Dan a long moment. "You do look Uncle Yitzhak. But he seem much older. He should retire by now. Did enough for one life, maybe ten. Always in trouble. You always in trouble?"

"Not really. Not until now. What'd your uncle do?"

"Tried to go Israel. So they force him quit job as chemist. Then they put jail as parasite. He refuse eat, first until he get Hebrew Bible for other prisoner, then until other released. Was in Soviet jail fourteen year, until glasnost. Now work for political prisoners across world."

"A brave guy. Where'd he get the strength?"

"From religion. Where else? … Are you religious?"

Dan shook his head.

"Of course not… That is why you need shaman."

Normally, Dan Gelber, a story teller by trade, would have gone deeper, would have given an expanded reply, but something about the subject at this moment made him feel oddly uncomfortable, almost ashamed. He would have been embarrassed to have told this woman how, the night of his bar mitzvah, he had attended a production of "Inherit the Wind" with its Darwinic theme and closet atheism, and come home to ask his parents whether they believed in God. He informed them, after they equivocated, that he, at the wise age of thirteen, did not. His religious "dis-history" went on from there. He was a child of his generation, secular to the core, at least in the way he lived his life, even with detours into Zen Buddhism (wasn't that really secular?) and other forms of meditation, again intended to fuse with a godless universe. Only in isolated moments was it otherwise, as on the Day of Atonement when he would begin the morning suddenly overtaken by the impulse to fast, but by ten AM would absentmindedly find himself in front of the refrigerator, having eaten a couple of spoonfuls of leftover pie and abandoned whatever paltry devotion he might have undertaken for that holiest of holidays. For a moment he would be guilty, but he thought it was more about his father's disapproval than anything theological. At least that's what Dan Gelber told himself. The other problem, or was it an excuse, was that, over the years, he could never find a synagogue he could tolerate. Either he would be lectured endlessly by a self-satisfied rabbi on the issue du jour or he would sit there endlessly in an orthodox shul, unable to comprehend the Hebrew while glancing upwards at the women's section, wondering if he had been transported into some medieval world of enforced patriarchy.

Still, the dilemma remained. What was it all about, Alfie? He recalled reading in school about Pascal's wager - that a rational person ought to live as though God existed. If, in the end, God is an illusion, you would only lose some temporary pleasures, but if he is real, you would have your eternity in Heaven instead of the decidedly irksome opposite. The French philosopher's gambit appealed to Dan intellectually, but far from enough to adjust his lifestyle accordingly. He was having too much fun in his daily existence or trying to convince himself that he was. It wasn't until he was older when he stumbled on that wager again and started to wonder if it was not indeed the wise way to live your life. But by then it was already too late. As with the leftovers in the refrigerator, he had already eaten his fill. There was no going back.

"Is amazing way you look Uncle Yitzhak." The woman, shaking her head again, interrupted his reverie. "You could be brother, even twin. Ashkenazi DNA, I see on Ancestry.com. Very small group. Many hate each other. Maybe too much inbreeding." She poured herself a stiff vodka and downed it. "Okay, I take you."

"Are you kidding?"

"No, no. I take."

"That's incredibly generous but… you certainly don't have to. It's a long way. Don't you have to work? What about your customers?"

"How you going to do this by self, naïve American alone in Siberia? They eat you alive. Tiger, wolf, shaman, tribesman with bow and arrow, jihad terrorist… yes, we have them…, kidnapping you for ransom and then beheading you anyway when it come - make no difference. …You need *protectsia*… You know Hebrew word? Does not mean protection exactly. Mean more like being connected to important people. You know – people in charge who can help you."

"You're in charge?"

"Not so much but pretend…. You can call me your connection."

Protection? Connection? There was something extremely weird about all this that Dan couldn't make out. Where did she come from? Why would she possibly want to do this for him? For all her refusenik talk, or maybe because of it, she could be in the KGB or that modern version, the FSB. That would be a connection, all right. There was nothing like being in Russia for making you feel paranoid. They spied on everybody. But what choice did he have? Dan knew he needed help. In fact, he was lost without it.

"What's your name?" he asked as he got in beside her in an aging Soviet Zil limousine that looked like a Chrysler Imperial circa 1962 with enough body rust to give tetanus to a medium-sized army. It backfired loudly, bouncing up and down, when she started up.

"Sonya Lieberman… like former senator," she said. She gunned the motor and the car sputtered, spewing what seemed like a couple of dozen gallons of oil before lurching forward.

They drove into the night only a relatively short time when, not yet even three AM, the sun began to rise again. They had been crossing a tundra with little vegetation, but the terrain started to dip and they were soon in the taiga of legend, tall Siberian pines surrounding them. They passed a series of wooden shacks behind stone walls that Sonya told him was where many political prisoners had been incarcerated and often starved by Stalin and continued on into a region of lakes dotted with granite outcroppings. It was eerily peaceful, despite other random decrepit structures, apparently remnants of the Gulag. Little streams crossed the road that had now narrowed considerably and was more rutted, making it difficult to negotiate. The Zil began to shimmy and Dan feared it would get a blowout or even fly apart. But nothing untoward happened. They crossed a wider stream that sprayed water over the windshield, obscuring their vision. The now-trusty Zil ploughed on through a clearing into another grove of pines. They were deep in the woods, the light suddenly dim. The road veered off to the right when a clump of fallen tree branches blocked their path.

Sonya muttered a curse and stopped the car. She and Dan glanced at each other and got out. Although the branches fanned out across the entire road, the tree trunk itself had remained standing and it was possible they could drag the breakage off far enough to the side to get through. They positioned themselves on opposite ends and began but it wasn't so simple. They struggled as if the branches were still tightly connected to the trunk, although they appeared to be severed. Sonya frowned, trying to figure out what the problem could be—it seemed illogical—when Dan noticed something moving behind her in the woods. He stopped and nodded in that direction.

"Bear," he said urgently while remembering to keep his voice low. He moved his hand slowly in order not to threaten the animal with sudden movements, just as he had been instructed years ago by a national parks ranger. He had only seen bears in the wild a half dozen times, mostly rummaging through garbage cans at camping sites. This one was clearly coming toward them. And quickly. Almost scampering. "Do you have a weapon in the car?"

Sonya shook her head. She was staring at the animal with a puzzled expression. "Not bear," she said.

"What is it?"

"Man."

The "animal" suddenly stood fully erect and walked toward them. Dan's mouth had dropped open, but he wasn't all that astonished, "I know him." Who else could the man have been after all, though anybody would have been hard to recognize through the ursine costume? "It's Nawang Gombo – the shaman I told you about."

"Perhaps he blocked road."

"Sorry to have caused inconvenience," said Gombo, close enough at this point to have overheard. "Did not want to miss you on way. Who is friend?"

"This is Ms. Lieberman. She is my… connection." Gelber was doing his best to stay calm, not at all sure he was glad to see Gombo under these circumstances. Or at least in this way.

"How do you do? Pleased to meet you… though I not sure what connection means," said the Nepali with a smile that was barely visible through the hood. "I have heard word used in relation to drug, but that unlikely definition in this case."

"Is just phrase," said Sonya.

She and Gombo were regarding each other warily.

"Why the bear suit?" Dan asked.

"In Siberia, necessary take precaution." Gombo pulled back the hood revealing a series of scars along his face and neck Dan had never noticed before. Some still oozed blood. "Wolves fear bear. Everyone respect bear."

"You okay?" Dan gestured to the gaping scratches.

"I fine," Gombo replied, walking behind the clump of branches and extracting from under the fur a long, curved knife that looked like it came from the wardrobe of Genghis Khan. "Nice fisherman bring me here but only can come so far. Then I put on suit to be sure. Not only for wolf. Many here for same reason you are. Not just to win next Slam."

"Eternal life."

"More than that. … You shall see." He tugged upward, revealing a thick cord wrapped around the main branch, securing it to a boulder. "Wise man have much to gain. Whole world even." With a guttural cry, he raised the knife high and cut through it, freeing the entire clump. Then he yanked the branches aside and gestured. "Now you can go. Plenty room even for big old communist car."

"Thank you," said Sonya, her voice preternaturally flat and affectless.

"Is my pleasure…. If you are so kind, allow me to ride with you. From here is quite dangerous. Even Russian government not come."

Dan glanced over at Sonya. It was her call. Dan was suddenly not too happy to have Gombo in the car with that knife.

"It would not be God's way to leave you here."

"Maybe not. I am not expert on that…. But thank you, missus."

"It's miss."

She got into the car, Dan in front with her and Gombo in the back.

"Where do we go from here?" Dan asked.

"Shaman live in village by dark lake. Many wolves protect."

Oh, great, Dan thought. "You've been here before?"

"More than once. Better herb here. Pure. Not so many tourist disturb nature like in Sagamartha. I show you."

Gombo pointed to the proper fork in the road and they drove North again through the woods. As the sun began to creep higher, Dan started to hear wolves howling, faintly at first, then louder. Didn't they only do that when there was a moon? And the weather was getting hot, almost like a Santa Ana condition—those desert winds, when, he remembered well from Raymond Chandler, "meek little wives feel the edge of a carving knife and study their husband's necks." Was he in Siberia or Los Angeles? He glanced over at Sonya, wondering again why she was doing this? Why had she volunteered to take him? Maybe she wasn't a KGB agent. He always knew, deep down, that was unlikely. Could she be interested in eternal life herself? She was a little young for that, but perhaps she was planning ahead. Of course, by the time she reached eighty, in another forty years or so, half the world would be turning bionic. She would have a more technological solution to life extension. Dan laughed softly at the grim irony of his pathetic pursuit. He was probably one of the last generations to be mortal in the old sense. Soon enough people would be replaced by high tech prosthetic devices, organ by organ, replete with brain implants to raise their IQs or minimize neurosis. At what point would they cease to be human? If man was made in the image of God, was God a cyborg? Somehow he doubted it, but then who knew? He also somehow doubted eternal life was Sonya's motivation. But what was it? Why was she put before him so fortuitously? Perhaps she was an angel come to save him - an absurd thought on the face of it. What had he done to deserve that? He was the one who had sought eternal life, or a second chance anyway, and had bought into it in the most casual thoughtless manner. In any Faust legend he was going to have to pay. Why fight it? The time had come. But what would be his punishment? Would he be beamed straight to Hell or eaten by a pack of wolves? At this point, it didn't matter so much to him, at least he wouldn't admit it did. He was a man well up in his seventies. He had lived a full life, with the normal ups and downs. Not only that, he had gotten that second chance and become an international sports sensation. Could anyone realistically ask for more? No, he was more than ready to meet the wolves, to put himself in their claws or jaws or whatever it was, although he hoped someone had a gun handy so he could put himself out of his misery before the lupine carnivores shredded him like so much pulled pork at a barbecue. Still, *finito commedia, ya basta*, he would be ready. Life had its pleasures but in the end living was overrated. He had had enough. Time for the big sleep, as the very Raymond Chandler famously put it. And just think - no insomnia. That would be a first. Yet he vacillated. At one moment he was scared of death, at another he welcomed it, almost like a bride. Nevertheless, there was no reason to be alarmed. He could get another swallow or two of this unknown herb, still somehow available in whatever quantity in godforsaken Siberia, and live to fight another day, perhaps even play in Australia next January in the first Grand Slam in yet another tennis season. It mattered not. None of this did. Everything was irrelevant— were it not for Molly and the children. That was like a ramrod of steel up his spine. He had no choice. He had to continue. Giving up was a luxury.

Now they were in a forest of Siberian pines so thick they obscured the growing daylight. Only isolated beams shot through branches like lasers. Dan could hear the wolves howling as if it were night. The air smelled bitter, pervasively acrid, like waves of marijuana cigarette smoke wafting through rock concerts. Soon what appeared to be swirls of dust blew up in front of the car. Crackling sounds could be heard in the distance. Were they campfires? Momentarily they seemed closer by. The howling of the wolves mixed with a chorus of cries of other animals. Suddenly a flaming branch came flying down from one of the pines, bouncing off the hood of the Zil. Within moments, trees were igniting all around them, embers spraying everywhere. A line of flames ran along the ridge in front of them as a second one darted across the road to an abandoned barn that instantly caught fire, its flaming roof sliding off and then crashing to the ground at the foot of the adjoining stables. Horses started stampeding. Yet another ridge went up in flames as embers cascaded like a fireworks. What was going on? A forest fire! Was he dreaming? Was he back in California? Was he hearing that shouting again? The siren?

"Always fires here," said Sonya, sensing what he was thinking. "Even bigger than yours. Last year burn seven hundred thousand acres. They have smoke Canada." Several figures dressed in colorful costumes, bright red and green, raced past, running for their lives. Some were pulling reindeer. "Mansi people. We must go back." She began to turn the wheel.

"No!" It was Gombo. Dan spun around to the Nepali who looked totally different. His face was devoid of the scars now or any evidence of them. All of a sudden, he seemed like a man in perfect health, almost ageless, as Dan had seen him in their first encounter. But there was something different, almost otherworldly. "Is not time to retreat. All herbs be gone. You have no hope for life. Only death. Never see wife and children again. This is last chance. Get herb. Live again."

Dan stared at Gombo. He could see the flames of the fire reflected in his eyes. The Nepali's mouth was slightly open with his tongue protruding slightly outwards in a serpentine manner. His incisors were sharp, like Dan imagined a Siberian tiger's.

"You are Mephistopheles."

"Western legend. I am Eastern."

"You led me here, didn't you? To Siberia."

"You wanted to come. You wanted more. They all want more."

Dan turned urgently to Sonya. "Turn back. Quickly."

"Not good idea, Mr. Dan," said Gombo. He raised his right index finger in the air. There was a flash of light. For a brief second, Dan thought he saw a television screen bolted to a wall. It was showing his old house going up in flames, the one he owned on Point Dume in Malibu years ago at the height of his screenwriting career. A reporter was pointing to it, while talking to a woman who was crying. Then the image was gone as a ball of fire exploded in the middle of the actual road behind the Zil, shaking the earth and creating a crater a hundred feet in diameter, making any return impossible. There was no going back. "Do not be alarmed, Mr. Dan," Gombo continued. "Is favor to you. You still have chance for eternal life. Young, old, it is but a cycle."

"I'm not interested, Gombo."

"Yes, you are. All are interested. Go forward, miss... You are miss now. See I respect.... Even you..." Sonya hesitated. A line of flames higher than the car was crossing not more than fifteen feet in front of them. "Just drive through. Like circus."

Sonya shrugged, hit the gas. At that second, the flames disappeared and the Zil zoomed through.

"Communist car not so bad," said Gombo. Dan did not laugh.

"Good enough for Brezhnev, good enough for the Devil," said Sonya.

This time Gombo laughed. "Brezhnev was idiot. Everyone know that... Go left at burning tree."

They were all burning trees, but there was only one dirt road to the left and Sonya took it. They arrived at a clearing surrounded by stones piled into pyramids. Just beyond, Dan could make out the shadowy image of a dark lake.

"Get out here," said Gombo. Sonya stopped the car and at that moment Dan had another flash vision of a television screen, images appearing like jump cuts in a movie - first a helicopter dumping water over burning hills, then a dog - a border collie - engulfed by flames followed by a child, a young boy resembling Zack running out of the smoldering wreckage of a house, tears streaming down his face as a firefighter grabbed him and hustled him onto a truck.

Dan was feeling short of breath and clutching his stomach when Gombo broke the vision. "In the middle of field is last growth herb. Rest up in smoke."

Dan got out of the car and stepped through the stones to the center of the clearing. The earth was bare. Gombo pointed to a lone scraggily tuft that had shot up like a weed not far from the center. "That is herb. It has no name."

Dan crouched down and examined the growth. It resembled a miniaturized clump of pampas grass of the type that grew all over California, that he had had in many of his back yards. Simple and mundane, so easy to overlook no one would ever guess what it was. It was almost predictably so. This was the fountain of youth that Ponce De Leon and millions of other people had spent their lives searching for.

"Go ahead. Take. You can have," said Gombo, nodding to the herb.

"You don't want any?"

Dan waited for Gombo to reply, but he seemed to have vanished. There was a silence that went on unnecessarily long. Dan glanced questioningly over at Sonya when someone spoke from behind him. The voice that answered was radically different.

"Not at this point. It's more efficacious that you have it in this particular instance." Efficacious? Gombo? The Nepali – if that's who it was – now no longer spoke in an Anglo-Indian accent but with the smooth, almost purposefully nondescript tones of a broadcaster for NPR or the BBC. Dan turned to see the man's entire physical appearance had changed. He stood before Dan as a Westerner, tall and athletic with just a hint of grey at the temples, dressed casually but smartly in khakis, tailored celadon shirt and a pair of suede penny loafers as if he were about to deliver a TED talk at Aspen. "Yes, it's still me. You know who I am. There are no secrets. There never should be. Transparency works best in the end most agree." He waved his hand and the fires stopped, the flames dying into embers and the smoke clearing almost instantly. "There... better, isn't it? Now we can talk like grown-ups and make some decisions." He looked down thoughtfully before continuing. "I have to thank you for coming all the way here. It's been some journey." He shook his head. "This is a remarkable opportunity for us, this moment.

You've been a great friend, Dan, but we should think about going further. It would be wonderful if you would join with me, with my movement. Not just for you, but for everyone, for humanity that suffers so much, too much. We need to help them abandon the ancient superstitions that only lead to violence and division and embrace the healing understanding of science, of proven knowledge, as it expands."

"I don't understand where I fit in in this?" said Dan, not entirely sure why he was asking.

"You would have a natural leadership position. Being a renowned athlete was but a gateway, a means to the far greater end of what you can do for others. After you are acknowledged as The Goat, already a virtual fait accompli, you will still be a young man. The potential is infinite—first spokesperson for your sport, then captain of industry, television personality, congressman - and then who knows - governor, senator, even president or international official at the United Nations or the World Bank. You wouldn't be the first of that level to join the movement. Many important people have worked with me in the past. Sports stars as great as Jesse Owens or Pheidippides of Marathon, political leaders of all nationalities, ethnicities and ideologies, Nobel Prize winners in every field, even saints." He smiled at Sonya, then took a step toward Dan within a foot or two of the clumped herb. The world was silent now, as if nature itself were hanging on his every word. "And I know you won't exploit those positions unfairly. You will work for the public interest whenever you can. I have read your books and seen your movies, am familiar with your life history and values. You were chosen for this, from the beginning. I have an interest in your being a good president or whatever you become in this life or the next, even a great one. My reputation is at stake. I am as concerned about my future influence as anyone. Our movement depends on it. So I won't ask you to do something untoward. Not now, not ever. I will shield you from any possible embarrassment as you pursue your goals… And I can assure you you will have Molly and your family as well as all the Mollys and families of the future you could possibly desire… So, my friend Dan, you do not have to die here, as legend may have dictated, be consumed by fire or some other imaginary cosmic force. That is the folklore of a more primitive time that you may easily bypass. Indeed, you have all your life." He reached down and snatched the clump of herb from the Earth. "All you need to do is ingest this bit of grass and go on to live this and many lives to come at the highest level. Consider it like a contract that I can guarantee forever. I am, in a sense, the ultimate subscription service. You keep re-upping and you never have to pay." He held the herb out to Dan. "Nothing to worry about. It tastes just like parsley. Go on, try."

"What happens if I don't?"

Gombo raised his hand again and the fire resumed in an instant, flames breaking out, branches cracking.

"I thought that was folklore," said Dan as the flames drew closer around him. He was already feeling the singe as some sparks landed on his pants. He slapped at them with his free hand. One had bored a hole in the denim, sending up an acrid smell.

"I don't want to deal with those traditions any more than you do. Or the punishments of an outmoded system that I have always done my best to undo. But you shouldn't let this concern you. You know what they say about guilt. It's a useless feeling that never makes you change your behavior. Besides, you had a good thing going. You weren't doing anybody harm. You were making people happy.... your fans, your family, your country. You don't want to continue? You came all this way. This is not an ordinary herb, like the ones in the Himalaya. It is unique. Once you have swallowed it, you are protected into infinity."

"By you?"

"Does that matter? It is the result that counts... But, if you insist, I have already said that I guarantee it. Look into my eyes and you will see."

He smiled at Dan and looked him straight in the eyes. Dan had trouble looking away, although he thought he should. He knew he was being deceived or hypnotized or both but, on some form of remote control or just from a lifetime of habits, the easy way, he reached out toward the herb. The tips of his fingers were shaking as he stretched for it. Around him he could hear the sounds of the raging fire, almost on top of him now. They were reaching fever pitch, punctuated by the desperate banshee cries of wolves and other animals, known and unknown. The forest was a veritable cacophony as, his fingers still shaking, his hand moved closer to the herb. And then he took it, the smiling Gombo or whoever he was opening the palms of his empty hands.

Dan looked over at Sonya who was studying him curiously, then stared at the herb in his hand when suddenly, without the slightest warning, he was surrounded by perhaps twenty Ugric tribesmen dressed in wolf cloaks and carrying long poled spears and guns. Their leader - a shaman in full regalia

- had an assault rifle. All the weapons were pointed directly at Dan's head. Dan gasped. The shaman said something in Russian.

"He wants you to drop vegetable," Sonya translated.

"Okay, okay, of course," said Dan, staring down the barrel of a gun and starting to release the herb.

"No, don't!" said Gombo sharply, stepping in front of the shaman while turning to his tribesmen with a firm "Nyet!" He took the assault rifle from the shaman who, realizing he was in the present of some kind of master, dropped to his knees. The other Ugrics, suddenly meek, immediately followed suit. He addressed them in Russian, then turned to Dan. "I explained that this… vegetable… has been reserved for you only. Anyone else who partakes will be punished severely. Now… it is time for us to welcome you."

He nodded to Dan, waiting for him to eat. The tribesmen formed a concentric circle to observe the ritual. Dan looked toward Sonya. "Is for you the decision," she said. "No one else. I cannot help you." He stared back down at the herb in his hand. It looked suddenly fresh and green and had the aroma of sweet grass on a summer's day. It brought back memories of his childhood, rolling around searching for the four-leaf clovers. He drew the herb closer to his mouth. He could almost taste it. What was there to lose? Everything could be back to where it was. In a matter of weeks, he would be in Australia, making preparations for the open. The whole family could be with him, staying at the Intercontinental Hotel in Melbourne, the same penthouse suite they always had with those fabulous room service pancakes the kids loved so much. Molly would always try to get them to order something more healthy, but they both hated Muesli. Who could blame them? He didn't like it either. The herb came closer to his mouth. He stuck out his tongue to try it. Closer, closer. But somehow it would not reach. It was as if the organ was trapped by a mysterious force, unable to move. Suddenly, he felt nauseated. The stench was amazing. He stared momentarily at the herb and threw it to the ground.

Mortified, Gombo lunged forward, grabbed the herb and came toward Dan as if to push it down his throat. Dan, surprising himself, responded by jumping back at him. Within seconds, the two men were wrestling, the herb like the gun in the hand of two combatants in a cowboy movie. Trying not to think of his age, Dan, mustering all the strength he could dredge up from his well-worn muscles, held his own momentarily, but Gombo, the stronger, ox-like in fact, finally succeeded in pulling Dan's mouth open and began to insert the herb down his gagging throat. The Ugrics gathered around to watch, a spectacle whose end they may already have seen. But with the herb halfway down his throat, Dan gagged and spit it out.

He summoned up the last of his energy and threw Gombo backwards. "I can't believe I listened to you, Gombo," he said. "What was I thinking?"

The shaman staggered for second, then gathered himself and headed for Dan like a battering ram. He lifted him up by the shoulders as if to hurl Gelber into the flames.

"Good-bye, Mr. Dan!"

"No, do not!" said Sonya, raising her hands with a confidence that was almost other worldly.

Gombo froze, staring at Sonya. She looked like something out of the early Renaissance, a portrait by Fra Angelico or Cimabue.

"That is forbidden, as you know."

The shaman started to back away. He seemed terrified.

"Please, Miss. Please, do not! Please!" he said, returning to his Anglo-Indian accent.

The Nepali dropped to his knees, hands clasped, continuing to importune her, "Forgive me! Forgive me!" but Sonya ignored him completely. Instead, she opened her arms wider still with her palms facing the sky. She threw her head back as if looking heavenward. The fires stopped instantly, no more crackling. The wolves ceased howling. The Ugric retreated into the trees, vanishing as fast as they had appeared. The forest was preternaturally silent except for Gombo who was sobbing.

Then an extraordinary white light, almost blinding, dominated the landscape, obscuring the forest itself as the sounds of a celestial choir rang out.

Squinting, Dan could just make out Gombo, crumpled on the ground, his head bent to his chest like a shriveled animal bathed in formaldehyde in a laboratory jar. Sonya turned to Dan and smiled. She picked up the remaining herb and handed it to him, nodding with a beatific satisfaction. It was for him.

XVIII
NOT YET

Dan Gelber heard a machine-like hum and a slow rhythmic pumping sound. Someone was talking dimly in the background. His left eye twitched and then the right one. The right had been the strong one. He had always been extremely right hand dominant, forcing himself to exercise the left with weights and kettle bells that often felt too heavy. Now the right was straining, as if about to open. He wasn't sure he wanted it to. He felt too tired. Better to rest. But the impulse continued. Finally, the eye opened a slit, so narrow his eyelash obscured much of his vision. He barely caught a glimpse of a tube attached to his arm, a television screen above him, a reporter talking among smoke-filled wreckage, the number of houses burned streaming across a chyron.

No, not this, not now, not yet.

He closed his eye again and kept it shut, lying there without moving, breathing as little as possible, willing the medicine, the serum, whatever it was still in his veins, to keep him unconscious, in a twilight zone so he could go back Orpheus-like to the world from which he had just come, a world of unfinished business.

After a bit, it was easier. His mind went blank. Exterior sounds subsided. All was quiet. He was asleep again.

Then he was driving along the Pacific Coast Highway in a rental car. Traffic was light. The temperature in the seventies. A California dream day. Somewhere around Oceanside he turned inland. In minutes he was at his

San Diego compound. A large moving van was parked out front, movers coming out of the house, carrying furniture and boxes. He wasn't surprised.

Dan got out of the car and headed up to the front door. He nodded to one of the movers and walked into the living room. Molly was standing there. She didn't look pleased to see him.

"Still an old man, I see," she said.

He was about to reply: Seventies are the new sixties, haven't you heard? But had the good sense to shut his mouth. He also didn't want to say what he knew now to be true, that he had made her up, the children too. "I could be young again, but that would be about the meanest thing I could do," he said instead. "How's your father?"

"He's in a coma now. Sepsis. I'm about to go see him. So if you'll excuse me."

"No, let *me* go."

"What?"

"I said please let me go. I can help."

"That's ridiculous. Are you a doctor now too?"

"You know I'm not a doctor. But there's something I can do. I went across the world for it."

"Across the world?"

"Siberia…. It can bring him back. Maybe he could even walk again…. I beg you let me do it. After that you can forget I ever existed. Do the same for the children. I made a dreadful mistake and can never be forgiven. Everything was about me. Everything. Maybe it's always been that way."

Molly looked at him, shook her head and exhaled. "I don't know why I believe you about anything… Intensive care unit. Scripps La Jolla Hospital."

"I would have loved you."

"What's that supposed to mean?"

"Nothing worth explaining."

In his present condition, Dan Gelber easily passed for somebody's elderly relative in the ICU. The nurse scarcely looked up as he walked down the corridor and into Hicks' room at the end. His coach was supine on a hospital bed, indeed in a coma. No one else was around. Dan glanced at the life support monitors. The patient's pulse rate was 24. Dan had read somewhere that your pulse should be at 60 bpm when sleeping. Of course, athletes could be lower but this was deep in the danger zone, edging toward flatlining. In fact, while he was standing there, the rate went down to 22.

"Coach, wake up! Coach!" he shouted directly in his ear. Hicks didn't respond. He didn't even twitch. "Look, I'm sorry I bugged out on you in Geneva. I know it was totally unprofessional and a complete embarrassment to you. But I wasn't afraid of Djokovic. It's just I.... ran out of gas is the best way to put it.... Wake up! Coach!" He tried again, this time near the top of his lungs, only restraining himself slightly out of worry the nurses would hear and run in. Still nothing from Hicks. Dan sighed, even though he hadn't expected a response. It was just an effort. "Anyway, not to worry. All is well. I brought your lunch." He reached into his pocket and took out an envelope. Inside was the herb, which he had ground down himself into a fine powder with a mortar and pestle. "Open up, old boy," he said, gently opening Hicks' mouth with his index finger and pouring the powder, which was less than a gram at this point, onto his tongue. Then he, equally gently, extracted his finger, closing the mouth. Dan waited. Nothing happened. Again Hicks did not respond. His jaw didn't budge a centimeter. He was frozen.

Dan looked around, spotting a paper cup by the sink. It was hardly hygienic, but he filled it and brought it over to Hicks. Even more gently, he opened the man's mouth again and poured the liquid drop by drop on his tongue where it mingled with the powder. Then he shut his mouth again and tilted his head back the smallest amount. Again nothing happened. But then, after a few minutes, the numbers on the monitor started to increase. The patient's beats per minute were in the thirties, then in the forties. Hicks raised his left hand slightly in the air, then reached up and rubbed his chin. He was at 56 bpms at that point. He opened his eyes.

"Hey, coach, how are you?" Hicks stared blankly at Dan whom he of course no longer recognized. "Everything's going to be okay. Get used to a new life. Maybe it's not coaching. Maybe you'll be playing again."

Hicks started to laugh.

XIX

WHEN WE DEAD AWAKEN

It wasn't until Dan heard the coughing that he realized there was another patient in his recovery room, even though said patient was only five feet away. It was a helluva way to come out of anesthesia, wondering if you were going to catch something as so often happened in hospitals. Also, the sound of the television above his head was suddenly excruciating. Was it the volume or was it the headache hammering at his temples?

"You have finally awakened, Mr. Gelber." It was Dr. Chung staring down at him. "We thought we had lost you for a while. Just kidding. Welcome back. We let you sleep longer than usual. Extenuating circumstances that began just as we were about to operate. Our anesthesiologist had to leave early. He lives in Thousand Oaks and had been told to evacuate. Luckily, he didn't lose his house. Or his patient… As you can see, you missed quite an event. It's been going on for some time." Chung gestured up to the television screen where flames were bursting out along a ridge, ambulances roaring along a road in front of it. "Get out! Get out!" a fireman was shouting.

"I think I saw it in my dream."

"You were dreaming? Many patients report that with the low-dose anesthesia we use now. But they forget it all within days. You might want to write it down. Good material for your profession…. What was the book where everything in Los Angeles was burning down? I read it in college."

"'The Day of the Locust.'"

"Yes, that's the one. It's always been the same in this city…. Anyway, I am pleased to tell you better news than others are having at the moment." He nodded up toward the TV, then glanced over at Dan's vital signs. "The operation was a complete success, at least from my perspective. You should be good as new again, relatively anyway. With any luck, and some serious physical therapy, you'll be back on the court in no time."

"Will I win Wimbledon?"

The doctor laughed. "I see you haven't lost your sense of humor. If someone wins Wimbledon at your age, they will have found the secret to eternal life. No harm in trying though. Someone's gotta do it." He tapped Dan on the shoulder. "We'll have you out of here in a jiffy."

An hour or so later, sooner than Gelber expected considering the well-known proclivity of hospitals, the door opened again. It was Amanda. He was surprised to see her, but also grateful and somehow relieved.

"Hello, sleepy head," she said. "I was worried about you. The hospital said you were breaking the record for recovery…. But apparently the operation went well."

"So they tell me. I haven't tested anything yet." He looked at her a moment, a bit overwhelmed by everything and still coming back to reality, whatever that meant. "Nice of you to come…. I hear half the city was burning down."

"Well, not quite. It always looks worse on the news…. They asked if I could drive you home, but I can call an Uber if it's easier."

"No, no…. I'd appreciate a ride, if it's not inconvenient…. Really."

She smiled. "That's why I'm here… I dropped some food at your house."

"Thanks… It's extraordinary. I had this amazing dream that wouldn't quit. You're not going to believe it…. You were in it. I owe you an apology."

She looked at him curiously.

"I refused to take you to the Himalayas."

Amanda laughed. "What a meanie."

XX

TENNIS, ANYONE
- THE SEQUEL

"Nice one," said Dan, although the shot wasn't that great, in fact was a mishit, ricocheting off the rim of the newly-purchased racquet and heading erratically towards the doubles lane. Gelber lunged to his right and, dipping down to his shoe top, deftly flipped the ball up for the boy who was surprised to see it come back and whiffed.

"Gee, granddad, how'd you get that? You're an awesome tennis player."

"Not so good anymore," he said with a self-effacing smile, meanwhile thinking you don't know the half of it. He knew better than to verbalize that. Actually, Dan Gelber was feeling pretty good, all things considered, only a slight pain in the glute when he moved to the right. He was far from ready for any serious matches, however, even on the senior circuit, not that that mattered any longer. His tournament days were over - real or imagined. They held no interest for him.

He took a step closer to the net. "Okay, now, Peter, here's a trick that will make you a better player than I am or maybe ever was." He held a ball up to the boy. "See the seams."

"Yes, I do."

"Good. Now I want you to concentrate on the seams on the ball. Nothing else. Don't think about whether you will hit a good shot or whether you will win or lose or whether you're a good or bad player or even your form… Just watch the seams like a hawk while you swing - all the way to the moment they meet the strings of the racket. Never look away. As much as you can, see the seams actually strike the strings. Your body will do the rest. Got it?"

The boy nodded, clearly apprehensive about whether he could do it.

Gelber wondered whether this was due to his condition or was the normal nervousness in such a situation, probably a little of both. He backed up and extended the ball in the air. "Don't forget to watch those seams," he repeated, remembering to do it gently and with a smile, not gruffly or aggressively as he had done with his father Zack when he was a boy.

Peter nodded again and squinted hard at the ball. Gelber flicked his wrist and hit the ball over the net. The boy swung and the racquet met the ball squarely, right on the sweet spot, sending it whistling over the net and bounding quickly toward the fence.

Gelber thrust his fist in the air. "Winner!"

Peter grinned ear to proverbial ear.

"Okay, that's it for the day." He put his arm around the boy as they walked off the court. "Magic, isn't it, watching the seams of the ball? Works for a lot of things in life, not just tennis." Was he sounding too avuncular, he wondered? There were lessons to be learned in everything. "Not that your granddad was able to do it," he added. "Not enough anyway. But I'm trying."

Later - after he dropped Peter at his therapy, ran some errands and then picked him up again - he took the boy to a local ice cream parlor.

"Don't tell your parents I brought you here," he said. "They'll think I'm bribing you with a sugar high."

"I can keep a secret," said Peter. "Anyway, they take me here too… Granddad, how come you moved to New Jersey? Mom and Dad can't figure it out. They said it's not like you."

Dan Gelber hesitated. "Well, they're right. I'm not like that, wasn't anyway. For a long time, I was too selfish."

"You were?" A look of disappointment flashed over Peter's face.

"Maybe I thought too much about myself. Wanted to always be the best best best at everything without thinking about others. But sometimes your unconscious… your dreams, if you're lucky and if you remember them… remind you of what's important…" Gelber smiled. "Like giving tennis lessons to your grandson. Other things too."

Peter frowned thoughtfully. The boy might have problems, Gelber thought, but he was clearly bright. Maybe the smart ones were always like that, too many synapses firing at once. Whatever the case, the therapy appeared to be working, at least to some degree. The kid seemed okay, on the right road. Dan Gelber wanted to help him stay there, to the extent that he could. He knew how easy it would be to wander. He had done it himself. Only now was he getting his first glimmerings of what was important. That desire to help Peter avoid those traps had brought him across the country. For some reason, it seemed the obvious thing to do after all that had happened. He wanted to keep talking, to explain more about life, as if he knew, or even tell the boy the story of Faust, Dan Gelber thought, glancing up at the spirit in the sky, whatever that was, but he felt he had already said too much. There was plenty of time. For now, and maybe for a long while, he should keep his mouth shut.

So they sat there a few moments, not saying anything, eating ice cream, when Peter finally broke the silence. "That woman who lives with you... She's not your wife, is she?"

"Amanda? ... No, she's not. She's a friend. And she's not living with me. She's just visiting." Dan looked at Peter who had maintained the same thoughtful expression all the while. He was getting an education. Or Dan Gelber himself was. "Maybe she'll stay longer. I'm hoping for that."

"Me too," said Peter, then he added "I'm glad you came."

THE END

ABOUT THE WRITER

Roger L. Simon is the author of thirteen books, eleven fiction and two non-fiction. These include the eight Moses Wine detective novels that have been nominated for multiple awards and translated in over a dozen languages. The first in the series, THE BIG FIX, was made into a film starring Richard Dreyfuss for which Simon, also a screenwriter, wrote the script. His other screen credits include BUSTIN' LOOSE with Richard Pryor, SCENES FROM A MALL with Bette Midler and Woody Allen and A BETTER LIFE. Simon was nominated for an Academy Award for his adaptation of Isaac Singer's ENEMIES, A LOVE STORY directed by Paul Mazursky. He has written articles for the *Wall Street Journal*, the *New York Times*, the *Washington Post*, the *New York Post*, *City Journal* and *Real Clear Politics*, among others, and appeared on talk radio and cable TV as a commentator. In 2004, he co-founded the pioneering online news and opinion website PJ Media and was its CEO for seven years. He is now its CEO Emeritus. THE GOAT is his first self-published book because Simon believes that is the wave of the future. A longtime resident of Los Angeles, he now lives in Nashville, Tennessee with his wife Sheryl Longin. He is a 4.0 tennis player - but only on that rare good day.